IN SIGHT OF FREEDOM

IN SIGHT OF FREEDOM

A Forgotten Trail on the Underground Railroad

R C Robotham

ISBN: 1508720320
ISBN 13: 9781508720324
Library of Congress Control Number: 2015903746
CreateSpace Independent Publishing Platform
North Charleston, South Carolina

Acknowlededements

No author writes a book alone. I will keep this brief and not include many writers who have inspired me over the years. That list would include numerous well-established, long-term favorites that surely others would list for themselves. Nor will I print a nearly endless list of new friends who are, like myself, new to this business and encourage each other to 'keep on keeping on' when the writing days get rough.

That being said, I have three special thanks I need to include in this book. It may seem like a cliché to some, but I thank my wife, Nives, for her endless patience and encouragement. Next I must thank two friends, who so often are mentioned together because they are twins. Their hours of editing, time spent teaching me better grammar, and endless notes and smiles of encouragement have been priceless. I deeply thank Jane Humphrey and Janet French. Without these people, this book could not exist.

PREFACE

JACQUES MARCUS BATEAU was born on July 4, 1836.
Led by his loving parents, Marcus and Victoria Bateau, his life would always be enlightened by the freedom star he was born under.

FREEDOM SONG

Follow, yes, The Dipper.
Follow, yes, The Gourd.
Sing that coded song to the Man
We's know fo' sure
"The Lord gonna trouble the waters."

By sea or trail, by wagon or foot,
Northward leads The Trail
"Bound for Glory" on the sail.

The Trail's alright when it's on the left,
Follow the graves 'round the backside hill
Fo' local folk scared of dem burin' grounds.

Folk not notice the SS sign,
Branded hand or branded post,
Follow the SS sign.
Gourds and steamers, trails, and such.
Gather us in yo' bosom, Lord,
For we's don't ask that much.

Anonymous

UP FROM THE SOUTH

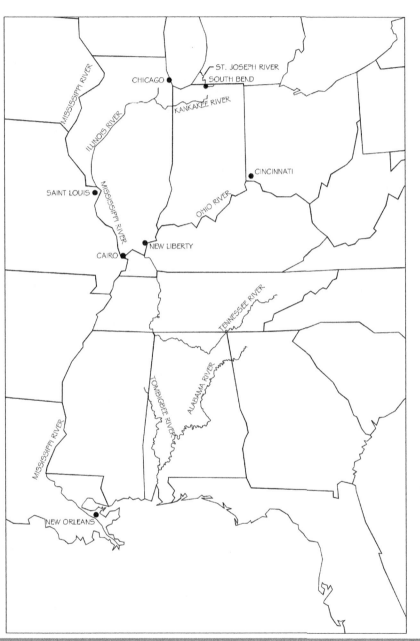

ST. JOSEPH RIVER
CHICAGO
SOUTH BEND
MISSISSIPPI RIVER
KANKAKEE RIVER
ILLINOIS RIVER
CINCINNATI
SAINT LOUIS
MISSISSIPPI RIVER
OHIO RIVER
NEW LIBERTY
CAIRO
TENNESSEE RIVER
TOMBIGBEE RIVER
ALABAMA RIVER
MISSISSIPPI RIVER
NEW ORLEANS

1

Young Jacques woke with a jolt! Rough hands had thrown him against the wall. The sleepy fog in his head cleared quickly. In fear, he crawled to the corner behind the chair. He covered his head with his hands awaiting another blow. But none came.

He heard another sound, "Whack, Whack!" and a low moan. It sounded as if some large hand hit what he assumed was his mother's face. She whimpered and then another "Whack." A man's guttural voice muttered, "You Nigger, slut!"

Jacques peeked around the corner of the chair. He made out the shadowy figures of two men. Each was holding a torch that lit the small space. He saw the man closest to him reach down and slap his mother who was now trying to protect herself with her hands over her head. The second man stood over Marc, Jacques' father, who sat rigid in a kitchen chair. The man hit him aside the head with something hard, maybe a gun or a club, but Jacques could not see clearly enough to tell.

"We know your kind, Nigger Lover! We don't like what you do, so let this be your notice. Your business here is closed. Most Niggers knows their place, 'scept that one." He motioned toward Jacques' mother still cowering on the floor.

Moving toward the door, the second man kicked Jacques' mother. The first man spoke roughly and spit at Marc.

"You'se can't get any lower than ya' all. Nigger Lovers ain't welcome 'round here."

With that, he hit Marc again with the heavy object, and Marc fell off the chair into a heap on the floor.

Leaving, the two men slammed the door, but it did not latch. Then as one final act of destruction, the men threw their torches into the shed outside. The last thing Jacques heard was one man's derisive laugh. "They'll never eat them for dinner."

The next sound he heard was a boat leaving the dock on the bayou creek. Then quiet - they were finally gone.

Jacques did not move. But Victoria quickly went to her husband. She reached for a rag and wet it in the sink bucket. She knelt and softly stroked his face, cleaning his bleeding head wound.

"What is that sound?" Marc asked, recovering his senses lost from the last blow. An orange light shown around the unlatched door. The unmistakable crackling of fire could be heard. Marc struggled to get up, but fell back on the floor into his wife's arms. Somehow, together they reached the door.

"Oh, damn!" Jacques heard his father mutter. He staggered to the sink and grabbed the bucket.

"It's no use," Victoria cried out.

"But I've gotta' try," he responded. They both went out and threw water on the burning shed. His mother was right; it was no use. Soon the smoky smells of charred wood and burnt chicken feathers permeated the house. Jacques lay paralyzed with fear. He began to recognize a growing rage in his gut that would motivate him for the rest of his life.

By the time dawn arrived, Jacques' mother had bandaged his father's head wounds. Her swollen left eye was visible evidence of the beating she had received. She had started a fire in the cook stove, and Jacques sat at the kitchen table sipping a cup of Chamomile tea. He had finally quit shaking from the fear. As his father entered, the reddening sunrise shown behind his outline in the doorway. Unwelcome as it was, the sickly smell of burnt chickens overwhelmed the kitchen.

"They're all dead," Marc announced. "The shed is completely gone along with all the tools. The good news is they must not have seen the boat behind the house. I'd concealed it with boughs for I was fearful of just such a visit." He came to the table to a waiting cup of tea and sat down heavily.

Victoria slid a plate with bread and honey to him. "Eat! You'll need all the strength you can come by."

They exchanged knowing glances. Jacques could see the hurt of their wounds and feel the hurt in their hearts, but more so, he sensed the strength of their resolve to go on. This too would be with him the rest of his life.

"We'll find another place. We will continue our work. I'll go up the trail today and share our misfortune with Mr. Ellis. He may have a suggestion for us. I believe we'll relocate closer to New Orleans. The work must continue."

He sipped his tea with a deep stoney look on his face. He glanced at Jacques, smiled weakly, and winked.

As daylight streamed in, Jacques saw a look of determination on his mother's reddened face and she nodded. "I'll pack. We'll be ready to go downstream when you return."

Jacques ate his bread slowly, realizing the seriousness of their words. He would help his mother and, together, the work would be easier. He stretched his arm to rub his head. It was then he realized he had a large sore lump, a tender reminder of his encounter with the wall.

Marc gave Jacques a nod as if to say, "You're the man here today." He gave Victoria a quick kiss. Her hand brushed his cheek as he grabbed his hat from the hook at the opened door. Hesitating, he looked back at Jacques, and said, "You help your mama. 'Je vous aime' (I love you both)," he said to them. With that he left.

It was getting very dark when Marc came down the trail out of the trees. Victoria smiled in relief. He came in and the three of them shared a hug. Relief and strength together were feelings Jacques would recognize and experience again and again throughout his life.

Jacques and his mother had pulled the boat to the dock. The few boxes holding their personal belongings were scattered near the door of their sparsely furnished cabin.

"We can be to the bayou fork in an hour. We'll know the way from there by the Indian campfires along the river. We'll meet Mr. Ellis, or his messengers, at the Glen Bayou dock around daylight and make more decisions then."

They quickly loaded the boat and made ready to leave. Victoria touched Marc's arm and spoke up quietly, "But how will we know which way to go?"

Marc smiled. "Chérie, n'oublie pas, L'Étoile Polaire." (My darling, don't forget, the North Star.)

As they all got into the boat, he reached over and tussled Jacques' hair. Jacques felt excitement for he knew for sure, *I am now a part of something big and important.*

⸺⟲

2

T HAT MOVE WOULD be only one of several young Jacques experienced. As he grew, his father, Marc, shared more of the work with him. Young Jacques learned quickly. Again, like their other camps, their new settlement was a cluster of three or four houses at a bend in the river, just upstream from an inlet stream of similar size. One of the smallest buildings sat in the center near the Y where the two streams came together. Jacques learned it was a lookout post where someone was assigned to monitor traffic on both streams. One of the youngest men, Alden, had no family in the group, and Jacques was pleased to find a special new friend. They would often sit with together and talk. Alden was small of stature for a young man, not much larger than Jacques. Jacques guessed he was nineteen or twenty years old. But everyone seems older when you are only twelve.

Because he was smaller than the others, Alden was often assigned to the small lookout cabin on the point. Jacques would go visit him frequently. Sometimes Jacques would take him food his mother had prepared. Alden was especially tuned to nature and taught Jacques to recognize many animal signs and bird calls. Jacques learned how to watch the water to determine how fast it was going. He learned how to watch the trees moving in the wind and determine the wind direction. Alden showed him how the wind affected the river.

Alden knew how badly Jacques wanted to go with the men on their trips. He encouraged Jacques, saying, "Learning these things will help you survive in the wild when you need to. It will make you more helpful to the team when we go out on our missions." Alden's advice gave Jacques confidence, and he mastered Alden's lessons quickly.

Jacques' father, Marc, was obviously in charge of this small group. Jacques listened to their hushed conversations and paid close attention. He began to recognize when the men were readying for a trip and took notice of what was packed in the boats, where and how.

One day, about a month after their arrival at the new base camp, Marc was preparing to leave with several of the others. Jacques helped them transfer gear into the two larger boats. His father seemed pleased with Jacques' willingness to lend a hand. Marc smiled and jostled his shoulder in an affectionate, man-to-man way. They both felt close.

Marc spoke to Jacques, "My son, you are growing, not just taller but stronger also. Keep it up, for you are a great help to me."

Jacques blushed and nodded, accepting his father's hard sought praise. He felt it was time to ask, "Father, can I go with you on this trip?"

Jacques and his father were carrying the last of Marc's gear out of the cabin, so Jacques' mother heard his plea. She gasped and touched her husband's arm. Their eyes met warmly but with a fearful realization. "No," is all she said quietly under her breath.

Marc stopped. Pulling her to him, he spoke quietly in her ear, "He's growing into a fine young man. I need to teach him well so he will survive. Soon he will come, but not this time."

Marc reached back for his pack and looked at his son anxiously awaiting an answer. Marc knew a simple "no" would not suffice, so he motioned to a nearby bench. He patted the seat indicating for Jacques to sit.

"You are correct, son," he stated. "You are growing and learning quickly. Yes, you need to come with us to master the rest of our procedures, the maps, and the routes. No, you cannot come this time." Jacques' face looked sad, and he stared at the ground.

Marc spoke up, "But, I will promise you can come with me when we go to Station Three next week. Would that be alright?"

Jacques' sad face turned bright. He glanced over at his worried mother, as did his father. Marc reminded Victoria, "Chérie, n'oublie pas, L'Étoile Polaire." (My dear, don't forget, the North Star)

Marc set off with the three others, each pair in a separate boat. It was dark as they left, and they were almost instantly out of sight in the blackness. Jacques' mother put her arm around her son. "Come in," she said.

Upon entering the small cabin, she directed Jacques to sit at the table as she reached for his writing tablet on the shelf. Jacques responded, quickly grabbing some matches. He lit the kerosene lamp in front of them.

"Tonight we must work on our lessons related to what your father just said, 'L'Étoile Polaire'. Do you remember? What do the English call it?"

"The North Star," Jacques proudly answered.

"And why is it we use the name 'Polaire'?" she asked.

Jacques recited what he had learned about the North Star's importance. How the North Star was useful for navigation in the Northern Hemisphere because it was positioned nearly over the North Pole. That fact made it appear not to move and always gave people a direction to true north. All mariners used the star to navigate their ships. With the star for reference, courses could be plotted on maps. Ships could sail easily in the proper direction, even when not in sight of land.

The lesson caused Jacques to daydream about the one time he had boarded a large ocean-going ship, several years previous when they were in New Orleans. He must have been nine or ten and had gone there with his father to get supplies.

"This is my son, Jacques," Marc said to his friend, the Captain. "Jacques, this is Captain Jonathan Walker."

"Nice to meet you, sir," Jacques politely replied and shook the Captain's hand.

"Captain Walker is a very important person in the movement of fugitive slaves. Being a sea captain, he has shown us how to use waterways, like the Mississippi River, for faster transport."

Captain Walker gave them a tour of his ship. At the helm, along with a compass and the big wheel for steering, there were charts and maps with lines. Even though they looked confusing, Jacques paid close attention. He asked Captain Walker several questions and was pleased to see an approving smile pass from the captain to his father.

"You have a smart lad here," Captain Walker commented to Marc. "I'll need an assistant soon. Perhaps he could come with me some day?"

Captain Walker and Marc laughed, but Jacques hoped he was serious about his offer. He had a feeling of delight just being on the ship. Maybe sailing could be his life's work when he grew up. Jacques recalled that warm feeling again as he and his mother sat at the table. He asked her, "Do you remember when father and I went onboard the sailing ship?"

Victoria nodded as she continued writing lessons for Jacques to study.

"I'd like to experience sailing like that some time. Do you know the captain's name?"

"Oui," his mother replied. "However, I only know him as JW. He is a very important link in our work here. He is from another state to the north. Massachusetts is his home, I believe. Your father knows him much better than I do. You should ask your father about him when he returns."

Speaking of Massachusetts reminded Jacques of the symbolic meaning of "being directed to the North." Jacques had learned from his mother that they and their friends were known as Abolitionists. It meant they were against the practice of slavery and would do whatever they could to stop it. More importantly, his mother explained how passionately they felt, so much so, they risked their lives helping fugitive slaves escape to the North, away from their slave owners.

"Mamman (Mama)? What is the French word for freedom? Father and the men talk a lot about the people we help 'getting on to freedom.' I guess freedom must be the opposite of slavery. Am I close?"

Victoria nodded and smiled, as she was pleased with the way Jacques made connections about their work. She reached up for another book, opened to a certain page, and turned it toward Jacques.

"Do you know what this is?" she asked.

"Surely, it is the French flag."

"And can you read the French motto underneath the flag?"

Jacques peered at it for a moment. "Liberté, Égalité, Fraterrité."

"Excellent!" Victoria encouraged Jacques. He was pleased and smiled.

"Now in English?" his mother urged.

Jacque was not sure. "I think it is Freedom, Equality, and … maybe 'togetherness'? I'm not sure."

"You did well, my son. Yes, the last one is 'Fraternity' or 'Brotherhood'. Now, you see how important freedom is to all people. We even put it in our country's motto on our flag."

"I see now why our work is so important --- freedom is for all people. Slavery is the opposite and needs to be eliminated everywhere."

"You are so right!" His mother smiled and gave him an affectionate pat on his cheek.

Jacques continued to think a lot about the importance of freedom. The work his family did to help people escape slavery was essential. Also it was obviously dangerous work. Jacques remembered the beating they had experienced nearly a year ago. "Nigger Lovers," the man had called his father and mother. Jacques couldn't understand the words but certainly understood the pain as he recalled the goose-egg he had and saw the scar on his mother's chin.

As his thoughts went back to that incident, there was a question he wanted to ask his mother. "Mamman, are we Niggers?" he asked shyly.

His mother turned her full attention to her son, for she knew he was thinking about big ideas, maybe too big for him to totally comprehend. She took a deep breath, thought a little, and spoke.

"Son, that is a word we do not use in our home. It is a nasty word that ignorant people use to describe people of dark color and African descent. The proper word to use is *Negro*. Now let me explain some about our family roots. You know your father is French Canadian from Quebec. French Canadians are mostly French people, sometimes mixed with the blood of native Indians. I believe your father's mother was half French and half Iroquois Indian, which makes him dark skinned. My family is from New Orleans where there are also a lot of French people. My people are usually called Creole. Creole people are a mixture of French, Indian (mostly Seminole), and Negro. One of my parents, my father, was half Negro and half Indian. I hope that helps you understand why you, too, have dark complexion.

"So, to answer your question, you do have some Negro blood in you, but do not forget, we are not *Niggers*. I don't want to hear that word from you again."

"I'm sorry, Mamman."

"Just remember to be proud of who you are. Your grandparents and parents are a mixture of many cultures. We are proud of each of these backgrounds. Don't be sorry for asking a good question. It is important for you to know where you come from."

Jacques' mind went back to the horrible men he had heard use the word, Nigger. They were crude and nasty, but the incident reminded him of the dangerous work his parents did in the name of *freedom*. A while back there had been a deep sadness in their group when, Alden, Jacques friend, did not arrive at their designated meeting place. Jacques was especially concerned because he and Alden had spent so much time together. Jacques remembered the many nature lessons Alden had taught him.

There had been much worry and many hushed conversations, but Jacques was very aware of what they feared. Two days later, Alden was found and brought home nearly dead. He had been tied to a tree with one of his wrists slashed. Alden survived and still helped on missions, even though he only had use of one hand. Jacques had spent much time with Alden as he healed. They had grown even closer.

Alden's experience brought home to Jacques the fact that Marc and the abolitionists took many risks and encountered many dangers. Their work was very important. Jacques talked about his concerns to his mother while she instructed him in his lessons. Victoria had gone to school and was teaching Jacques to write and cipher, as well as read. Reading material was hard to find. It was hard to keep books when they moved constantly. They had an old Bible, written in French, so

Jacques was working doubly hard to learn both languages. Hopefully, when his father went to the city again, he would bring back some newspapers for Jacques to read.

One night, with the chores done and the men gone, Victoria lay the books before them. She was writing a new lesson for Jacques, when suddenly he saw her stop writing in mid-sentence. She had 'that look' in her eyes which he'd seen before. She looked to the window, noticing the eastern sky was getting lighter. She sighed deeply and closed her eyes. Jacques saw her lips moving. He knew she was praying for the safe return of Marc and the others. Jacques also bowed and prayed he could someday be as strong and brave as his father.

3

THE SUN HAD almost risen above the trees. Jacques and his mother busied themselves by the fire.

"Your father will be hungry when he arrives," she spoke to reassure Jacques as she saw knew he was as nervous as she was. Jacques paced the water's edge looking first upstream and then down.

"Come. Gather some more wood," she called. "We'll have coffee ready. While you help the men unpack, I'll prepare some breakfast."

Jacques sighed impatiently and followed his mother's directions. He went to the wood pile behind the larger shed. When he reached the pile, he paused and noticed his canoe paddle hanging on the wall. His was the only one there now, for his father and the men had taken the others with them on their mission. They always prepared for emergencies and took several extra paddles in case one was broken or lost in the current. Jacques' father had explained to him how, even when careful, a paddle could slip from one's grasp and leave him stranded in the current. Often later, the boat would catch up to the lost paddle and it could be retrieved. But, until then, the extra one was invaluable.

His paddle was one his father found, presumably lost from another's canoe. It was very special to Jacques for it was his first paddle, and it had special markings. It bore several painted figures which his father thought he recognized as being from an Indian tribe that lived farther into the swamp, upstream from their encampment. Jacques caressed the paintings tenderly, maybe even reverently, believing they represent-ed a good omen or prayer for his father's safe return.

Jacques placed his arm-load of gathered wood near the fire pit.

"Merci bien, Jacques (Thank you, son)," his mother said.

"De rien (You're welcome)," Jacques answered.

Suddenly, they both stood erect and still, for they must have heard the sound at the same time. Jacques looked at his mother, and she mo-tioned him into the cabin.

She spoke in a hushed voice. "You, too, heard the paddles in the water. We'll hide in here in case the visitors are not friendly."

Victoria reached for the rifle by the door and checked to make sure it was loaded. They both stood silently in the darkness. There was a crack around the door and Jacques moved to take a peek. Victoria put her hand on his arm and restrained him and his curiosity. Next, they heard a boat or canoe scrape bottom as it landed. Jacques could feel his heartbeat quicken. Suddenly their faces brightened.

"Cherie? Jacques?" came Marc's recognizable voice. Victoria rushed into his arms, weeping from the tension.

"Oh, ma Cherie," Marc whispered and brushed the back of her head with his hand. He looked over at Jacques, standing close, and gave him a reassuring wink and a smile.

"Thank you for being the man of the station while I was gone. I see you are both safe. I worry when I am away. But I'm glad you both know how to use the rifle. You had no trouble, did you?"

Victoria recovered herself and affectionately pushed Marc's chest. "You worry? What about us? You are two hours late! See the sun above the trees? What can I do but worry?" She continued to affectionately berate her husband. "Come now, sit, sit..."

"First, Jacques and I will bring up the gear. Your men must do work before they can relax with your fantastic cooking. Come on, son." They smiled at each other. Victoria just shooed them off with a wave of her hand.

Jacques beamed with his father's recognition. They returned with the gear, ropes, the food bags, and the paddles. Jacques took the paddles and hung them in the rear of the shed. He glanced at the paintings on his paddle. He touched them and smiled to no one, just a private 'thank you' that the Great Spirit had guided his father and the men safely home.

When he returned to the fire circle, his father had already stowed his gear in the cabin. His mother had coffee and food ready.

"Come," Victoria said, "But wash your hands, both of you, over there in the bucket." With the spatula she was using to turn to cakes on the outdoor grill, she motioned toward the bucket. The father and son both dutifully followed her orders.

After they ate and the cleanup was complete, Jacques spoke first, "Tell me of the trip, Father."

"Yes, I will, son, and you must tell me of what you have learned while I was away. But we've been up through the night; we will rest first."

Jacques nodded and, moving to his bunk in the corner, he collapsed exhausted.

The sun was high in the sky when squawking crows woke him. He could hear voices outside, and he noticed he was alone. His parents had already left the cabin. He went to the door and peeked out cautiously. He saw his father sitting around the fire pit with two other men. They were talking with urgency.

"We must get to Station Three immediately and move the Cargo. I fear they have been followed," Peter spoke with urgency in his voice.

"I hear you," Marc replied. "I guess we have no more time for rest." A look passed between Marc and Victoria.

"I will have food prepared and packed," is all she said. But the look on her face was one of worry as she noticed Jacques standing in the doorway.

Jacques knew what his father had promised, and his heart beat quickened. *My first trip*, he thought, *tonight!* He smiled, quickly dressed, and joined the men at the fire.

"This is our newest crew member," Marc said as if he were introducing Jacques to Jonathan and Peter for the first time. "My son, Jacques, has learned the necessary skills to work with us, and he will be going with us tonight."

Jonathan, the older of the two men, stammered, "Don't you think it will be a bit too…"

Marc cut the conversation and motioned toward Victoria. The men understood a mother's worry. They put down their cups, stood, and thanked Victoria for the coffee.

"Merci, Madam," they said, touched the brim of their caps, and left.

Marc, Jacques, Jonathan and Peter met a bit later down along the river near the lookout cabin on the point. Jacques' friend Alden joined them as they sat on the logs conveniently set in a 'V' around Alden's small fire pit. There they discussed their plan for the trip to Station Three. Jacques listened intently.

"Jacques and I will take the blue canoe out first. Jonathan, you and Peter follow in half-an-hour with the larger canoe. It will be needed, for I believe four passengers will proceed with you on the second leg of the trip. Agreed?" Marc was definitely the leader, and the men respected him a great deal. That made Jacques proud.

The men nodded. Jonathan spoke, "We will take the larger basket of eating supplies, so the passengers will have food when we drop them later with Reverend Jones at the Way Crossing. Then, we will return, join you, and we should all be back here by dawn. Okay?"

They were in agreement and worked out the remaining specific details together. Jacques was filled with excitement but he did not speak up. He waited for his father's instructions. Marc and the men finished making plans and moved off to gather their gear.

There were several hours yet before dark, so they decided to relax before the long night's work began. "Come," Marc motioned to Jacques. "You gather the paddles. We will need six, including your special one." Their eyes met. Jacques felt his father, too, knew the special power in the paddle they had found.

"Yes, I will," Jacques responded, but then he stopped. He wanted to tell his father how he felt about the paddle, but he was hesitant. However, he was now more like a partner than a son, so he said, "Father, before you got home this morning, Mother sent me to get the wood. I noticed my paddle was the only one there. I touched the painting and sensed a strong presence of the Great Spirit. I felt peace, and I knew the Great Spirit would guide you home safely."

Marc listened intently. "You are growing up so fast. I am glad to see you are also growing with the Great Spirit. Never forget the Spirit is with you at all times. Be mindful, and it will never mislead you."

"I'll remember, Father," and Jacques went off to do his job. Marc looked up to see Victoria standing near. They shared a loving smile.

Victoria spoke. "You speak wisdom, my husband. We will all pray that the Great Spirit looks over you and Jacques. You will be safe, I know."

Marc moved toward his wife. "Cherie, you too speak wisdom. Jacques is nearly a man and a good one. He has learned all that you have taught him. We can be proud."

They fell into a warm embrace, feeling each other's strength was a key to their lives. It had kept them close, as well as safe in separation, for all their years. They planned to continue that tradition for a long time.

They enjoyed the evening meal of fish, bread and greens. They watched the sky as it darkened. They welcomed the darkness as their friend for it cloaked them in safety for their work.

Victoria was sad and scared to see Jacques getting ready for the journey. He acted so old, so strong, truly his father's worthy partner. But... she pushed her fears away and promised herself, *absolutely no tears* at the departure.

Marc noticed Victoria and surely sensed her fear. He motioned to Jacques. Jacques hesitated at first, but caught on that it was okay. He went to his mother, hugged her, and reassured her that they would be all right.

"Remember what you taught me, maman. 'N'oublie pas, L'Étoile Polaire' (Don't forget the North Star). We are always guided by it, and we will return safely."

She forced a smile and let her son, becoming a man, go on his first mission. The darkness covered them as the two boats disappeared around the bend heading north.

Everything was quiet as they moved through the darkness on the water. Jacques marveled at how his father knew every turn, every overhanging tree, and every small inlet. Marc pointed out these things, teaching his new partner the importance of each sign. Jacques was very attentive and tried to take it all in. He remembered all that Alden had taught him, but the sounds of the night river were different. Marc explained how the different sounds also were signs.

Suddenly, Marc signaled silently and pulled the canoe up near the shore. They pulled under a cloak of branches and waited. Soon Jonathan and Peter pulled alongside in the larger boat. Jacques was confused and wondered, *What are we waiting for?*

After a pause that seemed to be many minutes, Marc tapped Jacques' shoulder with his canoe paddle. Whispering, Marc spoke, "Look ahead, just to the right of the big tree shadow."

Jacques peered into the darkness. He could see the tree shadow his father spoke of, then, but what was that? He turned back to his father. Jacques could see his father motioning and signaling to the other men.

He whispered to Jacques. "The lights, son. We are looking for two lights being lit to show us it is safe to proceed, and only one is lit now."

They proceeded, hugging the shore on around two or three more bends, quite a distance past the big tree where they first saw the light. There Jacques saw two lights on the shore, and both canoes quickly landed. There was very little talk, for silence was a code of their work.

Jacques helped load the four passengers into the larger canoe. They had minimal personal items. People don't carry much when they're running from the law. The last passenger appeared to be an older woman, and she moved more slowly than the others.

"I's a commin'," she whispered. She took Jacques' hand as she stepped into the canoe. She stopped suddenly. "You is so young, Son. You be blessed and safe tonight." Then she touched her finger to his forehead. Someone spoke. "I's a commin'," she said again. She got down in the middle of the boat with the others. They pulled a tarp up over their heads. Marc pushed the larger boat out into the stream.

"Au revoir (till we meet again)," he said to Jonathan and Peter as they and their precious Cargo quickly disappeared into the darkness.

Jacques secured their canoe as his father had taught him.

"Come," Marc motioned. "We have to work quickly to clean up."

Jacques listened to his father's whispered instructions. They needed to brush the ground to remove all tracks and any other signs that someone had been there. They dug a hole behind a tree and buried the few charred wood pieces and ash remaining from the fugitive's minimal fire. As the final task, they brushed their way back to their canoe. They splashed some water and removed the grooves where the canoes had been pulled ashore. Marc surveyed the area and nodded to Jacques that all was well.

Suddenly, Marc stood straight and still. Jacques was confused. Then Marc motioned to hurry, and they waded into the water pushing the canoe back downstream a short distance under a large overhanging tree.

"Quickly, tie all the gear bags to the canoe thwarts. Hurry, we don't have much time," Marc urged.

When that was finished, Marc pushed the canoe as far under the branches as he could. Jacques paid close attention, but he was worried about his father's obvious concern. Something was wrong!

Marc directed Jacques to step beside him into the river on the same side of the canoe. The water was chilly and nearly up to Jacques' waist. He had to be careful not to lose his balance in the current.

Marc gave directions, "Hold onto the edge of the canoe. Now lift it and help me turn it over, but be especially quiet. We will hold it and stay under it out of sight."

Jacques was really confused, as well as frightened. Both father and son stood in the water huddled together near the middle of the overturned canoe. Luckily, the current was slow near the bank, and it was easy to stand. Marc nudged Jacques and put his finger to his mouth in the universal sign for quiet.

Jacques heard a noise, then a voice.

"Damn, no one's here. Don't look like anyone's been here for a long while, neither."

A second voice responded, "Dang, I was sure this was the crossin'. I hid out over there two weeks ago when a canoe came and went in the night. I was dead sure them runnin' slaves were coming here."

"Oh, I don't blame ya none. There are so many trails and turns in this swamp, I'm surprised we even found this place. Let's take another look around just to be sure."

Jacques and Marc could hear noises as the men searched through the brush around the landing. They held on tightly to the canoe, almost not breathing, trying not to make any sound or movement.

Then they heard a voice, closer this time. "Well, looky here. Maybe we're too early and this here boat was left to help 'em in their escape."

"Ya may be right, Jake, but I promise you they won't be gittin' much use outta' this here canoe."

Then came a deafening sound. BANG! BANG!

"That canoe won't be helpin' nobody escape with those holes in it. Come on, let's git outta here."

4

THE VOICES MOVED off quickly. But Marc and Jacques waited for what seemed like an eternity. Finally, Marc nudged Jacques. Jacques was sure he was numb from the water or dead from the gunshot, but Marc's touch revived him.

Slowly, they lifted the canoe off themselves. Marc moved to the front and whispered, "They sure tried to mess us up this time. Come help me move the canoe over to the landing."

Jacques helped Marc pull the canoe up onto the shore. They both investigated the two holes with their numb fingers. Dawn was barely breaking, but the canoe looked like a disaster to Jacques. Jacques was slowly starting to get feeling back in his hands and legs when he heard Marc's say, "Wait here. I'll be right back." Marc disappeared quickly into the brush.

"*What?*" Jacques thought. "*Back from where?*" Jacques nearly panicked as his father disappeared, leaving him alone in that dark, scary place. *What if those men return?* He could feel his body shaking. He was not sure if it was from the cold or from the fear. Then, he forced himself to simply do as his father had taught him, to trust him and do as directed, *Sit quiet. Wait patiently.*

Jacques sat on the edge of the canoe and became aware of every small, strange sound in what he had previously thought was a silent woods. He could hear the gurgle of the water as it ran past. A quick splash, which he thought must have been a fish, startled him. He noticed the tree frog's sound, first over there, then nearer. It was a mating call. He had been taught that by his friend Alden back at camp.

Then he heard a twig snap. He hunkered down beside the canoe trying to stay alert. He cautiously peeked over the edge of the canoe hoping again that the two men had not returned. Nothing. Then another sound, behind him this time; he heard a familiar bird-like whistle. He smiled, for that was an old signal between him and his father. He whistled back.

In another instant, Marc was there beside him. Jacques was relieved and laid his head on Marc's shoulder. "It's okay, son," Marc assured him.

Both noticed the eastern sky getting lighter. L'Étoile Polaire was dim now; morning could only be a short hour away at most.

"There," Marc said washing off his hands in the stream. Jacques paid close attention and learned another important lesson from his father. Marc had returned from the woods with some pine pitch and some thick moss. Marc used the moss to fill the hole, pulling the splintered wood together to hold it all in place. He then smeared the pine pitch over it on both sides. He had to go out one more time to get more pitch, and that time Jacques was not scared.

"That should get us home," Marc said in a low voice as he admired his work in the growing light of dawn. "You remember this, Jacques, for it is a valuable survival technique."

Jacques nodded in agreement.

They righted the canoe and stowed the wet gear. They brushed away all trace of their work around the site, got into the canoe, pushed off, and waited. Marc looked nervously upstream. Jacques knew he was anticipating Jonathan and Peter's return at any time. It seemed like just a minute and, right on time, they came quietly paddling to the landing.

Marc and Jacques eased the wounded canoe into the current, and both boats moved on toward their settlement. As they neared home, the sky was lightening. Marc turned to Jacques, "The less said to your mother about the bullet holes, the better. Understand?"

Jacques caught his father's eye in the dawning light. Both smiled and winked. Jacques was proud, for now he knew his father thought of him as a man, a partner. He was even a partner in their secrets.

In the following months, Jacques grew and grew. He joined his father on many trips. The months turned into years as Jacques approached his eighteenth birthday. They had moved on from their settlement for fear of being discovered. The new camp was again on the river, also at a fork, and they made it home as best they could. There was not a lot of time for 'home-making' as their missions seemed to keep them always on the go.

On one trip Jacques went in the big canoe with one of the other men, Burt. They had picked up three people, a man, woman, and a baby. They had paddled on for several hours in the dark. The man passenger could see them struggling; Jacques' shoulders were aching. The passenger got up to help, for three paddlers would make better time. Finally, they slowed as they approached the bend which was to be their destination. Burt was being very cautious, and Jacques had learned to pay close attention for signs. They both saw the single signal light about the same time, but did not proceed. Burt slowly steered the canoe over to the opposite shore, and they passed the spot quickly.

After about a half an hour, they spotted the two-light signal and stopped. Jacques listened closely to Burt's explanation. Jacques remembered his father had explained the meaning of the one light signal: *It was not safe to stop.* There needed to be two lights to indicate safety. One of the men at the new downstream site told them that a stranger on horseback had ridden into the original landing. He had asked a lot of questions, saw that the two men there were just fishing, and wished them luck as he rode back into the woods.

The "station masters," as they were called, had properly hidden away their Cargo of persons. They had successfully camouflaged their site as simply a good fishing spot. But someone knew how to get to that spot, so the station master decided to move the landing site. They went to the alternative location, and there they put out the two-light signal. That is why Burt knew it was safe to land.

As time passed, Jacques friend, Alden, in spite of his bad hand, helped Jacques in unexpected ways. He taught Jacques how to use a compass. They talked of maps, the trail maps mostly. One day Alden handed Jacques a different map. Jacques unrolled it carefully and laid it on the flat surface of the table, smoothing it out gently. They held it in place with a couple of fist-size stones.

"What is this?" Jacques inquired, not so much as a question but more like a challenge to himself. Alden smiled but did not jump in with an answer.

Jacques observed, "This part is labeled 'Orleans' and over here is 'Seminole Land.' Oh, yes, that would be the land of the Seminole Indian tribe. I learned about them from my Mother. Yes, 'Land of the Seminole' was renamed 'Florida' by the Spanish. Ah ha! I think this is a sea-faring map. These lines must be courses of rivers, and these smaller lines must tell about the shape of the bottom."

"They tell the depth of the water," Alden interjected.

The two studied the map for a long time. Jacques had a dozen questions, and Alden did his best to answer from what he knew. Jacques felt a new sense of excitement. He was thrilled at seeing and studying a real sailing map. *Might I ever get a chance to use such a map one day?* He asked the question to no one, but his mind was already racing away on a sailing ship.

5

JACQUES BECAME A fixture at the camp. Sometimes he went with his father; sometimes he didn't. He did whatever was needed. He had to learn to take orders and do what was best for the mission, not just what was most pleasing to him. Sometimes, his job was as the lookout keeping watch for unwanted visitors. That was boring work, but he dutifully did it, even when he would have wished to be out on the water with the canoes.

He knew how to handle both the regular canoes and the larger one as well. The French trappers and traders had developed this larger canoe, a Voyageur. It could haul a large cargo of freight goods and /or people goods. Most often four men or more were used to paddle this craft. Jacques continued to believe his paddle with the paintings carried *good medicine* as his French-Canadian father called it. It was power to Jacques; it and his growing muscles gave him the power to move even the oversized Voyageur.

Marc called Jacques out to the group camp fire one evening after everyone had finished their evening meal. The men were planning the next big project. This system they called "the Underground Railroad" was careful to not use the same trail or the same stops every time. Their group had been resting up for a week after two long journeys.

Marc started by explaining they actually had two tasks to accomplish, and the men would split up this time. One group Marc would lead with the two smaller canoes. Burt would lead the second expedition using the larger, Voyageur canoe. Jacques would be glad to be with either crew, but he assumed Marc would want him with him. Jacques nearly jumped when Burt rose and told Marc directly, "I'm hopin' you'll send Jacques with me this time."

Marc looked at Burt for a long moment. Then, turning toward Jacques, he said, "Burt, I guess you'll have to ask Jacques."

Jacques was one of the men now, and he did not want to act like a kid and jump for joy. Jacques looked at Burt, then spoke to his father. "I will go with the Voyageur if you don't feel you need me with you."

Marc knew how excited Jacques would be to go with Burt, but he too played this man-to-man. "Son, Burt needs you this time. I'll get by."

Jacques walked over to Burt and shook his big hand. Only then did a grin of excitement show on his face. Burt put his big hand on Jacques' shoulder and squeezed it. Jacques pushed his hand away as if annoyed, but all knew he was pleased.

The next evening, they left. Burt, Peter, Henri, and Jacques were in the Voyager giving them four paddlers anticipating a heavy load of Cargo. Marc and Jonathan were in the smaller canoe. They stayed together until the first Y in the stream. When lights blinked a silent signal, the Voyageur was directed left in a westerly direction. The stream was easy with few curves and no trouble. They slowed under a bridge and stopped in its dark shadow. They dug their paddles in vertically to hold the boat against the especially swift current under the bridge. They both heard the sound about the same time, and they eased the boat farther into the shadows as the sound of voices came closer. The talking was accompanied by the clopping of a team approaching the bridge from the left. The team pulled the wagon over the bridge and passed right above their heads. Dust and sand sifted down on the party, but no one dared sneeze or spit. After it was gone, Burt gave a signal to move on.

They had only traveled about ten minutes when they again dug in and stopped the canoe. Burt raised his voice in one of their patented owl-sound signals. They all listened, but no response was heard. Another tense ten minutes later, Burt tried again, with a slightly different call. All ears strained to hear.

The sound was off to their left; it did not sound close. Burt answered and got two quick replies. He nodded to Jacques and Peter who pulled their paddles and headed out sharply. They often had to hurry at pickup points because being slow could mean capture or worse.

They soon heard the signal again, closer. Around the next bend two lights signaled it was okay to land. Pulling onto the shore, Jacques was surprised to see a team of horses and a hay wagon piled high. Although confused, this was no time for words or explanations. One of the men on shore, someone who believed as Marc did, patted the side of the wagon and a rear gate dropped down. In the darkness, figures emerged from under the pile, quickly brushed off some remaining hay, and hurried to the canoe. There were seven people in all, a big load. That meant hard paddling ahead.

Quickly they scrambled aboard the large canoe with their few personals. Jacques was standing half in the water helping persons board. The last person seemed to move with some difficulty and was urged on by the others. As the older man stepped into the water, he slipped and threw his weight against Jacques' strong arms.

Looking up into Jacques' face, he whispered, "Why, you'se just a child. God bless you child and keep you safe tonight."

Then the man surprised Jacques for, taking ahold of his hand, the man held it pressed to his chest. He mumbled a few words Jacques could not understand. Jacques assisted him into the boat and when all were covered, Jacques jumped to his paddling position.

He could not recall much of what happened next. He did recall how his body tingled and felt very warm, especially where the man had touched him. He noticed, also, that his paddle seemed to have a special lightness; it, too, was warm and sliced the water with a special power. He knew somehow he had been especially blessed.

They paddled for a long hour, and although the load was heavy, it went by quickly. Anticipating a heavy load, having four paddlers helped greatly. Jacques remembered that his first outing, with only himself and Burt, had been very hard work. He was stronger this time, but that was not all that made this trip easier. He and his paddle had been blessed.

It was easy to note, even in the dark, that the body of water grew significantly wider and, rounding a point, he noticed a large ship with numerous lights. He was so taken by the new surroundings, he did not notice the signals pass, but the Voyager swiftly left the protection of the over-hanging foliage and hurried double time out to the waiting ship, a large steamer.

There was a strong wind, and they pulled hard on the paddles to make headway. The waves tossed the large canoe to and fro giving everyone on board concern for their safety. Jacques heard a voice from under the cover and was sure someone was praying. As they came alongside the steamer, a sudden wave pushed them hard into the iron hull. The sound of a loud "crack" gave everyone a start, but the great Voyager held together.

Alongside and secured, the cargo of seven quickly moved onto the ship; the older man was the slowest and the last. Again, no time to talk, must hurry, but the man's flashing eyes caught Jacques' glance. They locked eyes for a short moment, then he was over the side and gone onto the boat and on to freedom.

The Voyageur swiftly moved back into the foliage cover from where they'd come. There they rested and shared some food Victoria had packed for them. Jacques was still a bit shaken and confused by his experience. He moved silently over near Burt. Burt did not respond until Jacques simply said, "I don't understand."

Burt smiled and explained this new transport and shipping method. This larger boat, the steamer, was going north up the Mississippi River. Jacques was excited to watch the larger ship move away quietly with only the faint smell of smoke lingering in the air. His mind expanded as he thought of being on a boat like that someday.

"But who...and from where?" Jacques stammered.

Burt put his gnarled working hand, which now felt smooth and comforting, on Jacques' shoulder. Then he spoke. "Do you remember going with your father to New Orleans several years ago? You went on a boat even bigger than this one we just left, I'd guess. Your father's friend was Captain Walker, but most just call him JW. He has setup a series of steamers used to help our mission. This was one of JW's smaller steamers. Still, it is able to transport more Cargo than we can. It can carry cargo all the way north, even to Chicago.

Jacques reeled around. "To Chicago? Wow! That would be a wonderful trip."

For some moments in the cool darkness, Jacques' mind was in a different place, on a different adventure, and on a very large boat.

6

T HE TRIP HOME in the Voyageur canoe was uneventful. The men
had hidden during the day deep in a wooded cove. They covered
themselves with tree bows and slept, for they were exhausted from the
long night's work.

As darkness came, they took off and returned to their base camp
just after dawn. As the Voyager neared home, it seemed strangely quiet,
and Jacques noticed Burt was instantly on guard. They did not land,
but purposely floated silently on past and landed a short distance away.
They quietly stowed and tied the Voyageur. All four men made their
way back toward the base camp area. Jacques then noticed something
that caused him deeper concern. He saw Burt and Peter retrieve pistols
from their gear. Now he was worried.

They made their way quietly out of the woods up to the camp from
behind the largest shed. They noticed that all the paddles were gone,
indicating that some canoes were still out. Marc and Jonathan should
have returned first. But no one was there. Something was wrong.
Where were they?

Coming around to the front of the cabins, they quickly inspected
each one, but each was empty. Jacques' mother and Burt's wife should
also have been there for they never went out on missions. That worried
them even more. The men looked for clues, but there seemed to be

no sign of trouble, no sign of struggle, and no other sign of anything unusual. Ideas swirled in their heads. Maybe the women had been abducted by local vigilantes or even the sheriff. They knew both women were armed and would use their weapons if they were needed. But where were they?

Just then they heard a canoe approaching, so they hid in the shadows. Soon, in the gathering light, they saw two canoes. The crews were their own partners and the women were with them. Jacques, Burt, and the others rushed to help them ashore. Everyone looked serious, and Jacques began to feel a pain of worry and anxiety well up in his gut. He rushed to his mother, helped her out of the canoe, and they fell into each other's arms.

They held each other and Victoria began to sob.

"What is it, mother? Please tell me."

"It's your father. He's missing. Last night after he and Jonathan returned, he insisted on going out on foot to check another landing spot. We just went to the nearest station to check, but we found no sign. There is nothing we can do now but wait. Come, we'll get some food for the others. We'll talk more later."

As if in a trance, Jacques helped with the canoes. They retrieved the Voyageur and brought in the gear. Each man took care of his own things as Jacques gathered the paddles. He carried them behind the shed and stowed them where they hung. His second load contained his personal paddle with the Indian paintings. Jacques stopped and began to sob quietly. He moved out of sight of the others. As he touched the sacred paintings, he spoke through his tears. *Oh, Great Spirit, guide and protect my father. I'm so scared. I must be strong now, especially for my mother.* He gathered in his emotions, wiped his eyes on his shirt, and joined the others.

Everyone was quiet and moved about mechanically, doing what was needed. After eating a hurried meal of bread, some cheese, and coffee, they fell onto cots exhausted. The sun was rising as they all sought needed rest.

Jacques awoke with a start. Maybe it was a dream, for he thought he heard his father's voice. But how? What he clearly heard were his mother's quiet sobs; he went to her, knelt by her bed, and stroked her hair. She turned toward him. "Oh, son. I fear the worst. I know you are near a man; I'll need you even more now." They held each other and cried. Suddenly they heard a shout from outside their cabin and rose to see about the commotion.

While Jacques and Victoria had been resting, Burt and Jonathan had returned up the river to search for Marc in the daylight. It was dangerous to move about at their secret stations during the day, but searching in the dark was fruitless, so they took the chance.

Burt's wife, Gloria, was the first to spy Victoria and rushed to her. "I'm so sorry. I'm so sorry." She sobbed and the two women hugged.

Burt came over to Victoria. Putting his big hand on her shoulders, he said, "We found Marc's body near Station Three. His hunch must have been correct. Someone must have discovered that landing spot. He must have stepped in a snap-trap set in the water, and it pulled him under. He must have drowned struggling to get free. Victoria, you know he was such a brave leader. We will all be lost without him." The three sobbed together.

Jacques moved toward the river where the men were removing his father's body from the canoe. Later, he would be grateful the body was wrapped in a tarp. His last view of his father would not be of him swollen and distorted. Peter and Alden gently led Jacques away to the fire pit where they all sat and grieved their deep loss.

The next few days were a blur for everyone. They prepared the body in a crude casket. It was decided to bury the body on *Isle Polaire*. The locals called it that because it was shaped like a compass with a projection to all four directions. The longest spit of land pointed north, thus they called it *Isle Polaire*, referring to the North Star.

After the burial, members of the team gathered for a group meeting. Decisions needed to be made and made quickly. In the network of moving the fugitive slaves, they could never keep the same routes for long. With Marc's death in the insidious trap, it was obvious someone must have discovered their latest routes. It was agreed that all had to be dismantled and the group disbanded. Burt and his wife would take half the crew and go join another team that operated farther north. Several of the single men would go off to join other groups operating nearby. Victoria, Jacques, and his friend, Alden, would return to New Orleans. Victoria's family lived near there, and it was best, for they would be safe there.

Secretly, Victoria had a special plan for Jacques. She quickly penned a letter to her friend, Captain Alex Hoover. She pulled Alden aside and gave him the letter. Her whispered directions were a mystery to Jacques, but he knew his mother always planned ahead. He was not surprised when Alden disappeared with one of the boats that left that evening.

7

THERE WERE TEARS and hugs as the group members separated for their respective new assignments. Burt came to Jacques and motioned for him to follow. They walked off a distance and both sat quietly on a log by the river's edge. Neither spoke, but it was a time of intense feeling. After an unmeasured silence, Jacques heard his mother call his name. He looked toward Burt, and Burt spoke haltingly, "Your pa was a great man who taught us both all we know about how to survive in this here dangerous work. Now you's a man and I know he's mighty proud of you, son. I don't know what to say, but..." Burt stopped, looking at the ground as if the scripted next sentence might appear there.

"Yes, Pa was my hero," Jacques stammered through his emotions. "But know that you've taught me a lot, too, Burt. I'll be forever indebted to you, and I'm going to miss you terribly."

There alone, they hugged, both teary.

"Jacques," came Victoria's voice a second time.

"You work hard, son, take care of your ma, and most of all, make your pa proud." Those were Burt's last instructions.

"Yes, I will, for sure."

Returning to the group, they were met with whispers and smiles. Bert and Jacques shook hands. Then Jacques helped Victoria into the canoe.

The settlement camp was soon just a small clearing in the vastness of the stream-laced wilderness north of New Orleans. All trace of their being there was gone. Personnel had disbursed to new locations to carry on the work. Victoria, Jacques, and Alden were the last to leave. They traveled a short distance following Victoria's directions. Jacques knew exactly where his mother was headed.

Before long, they pulled ashore at Isle Polaire. Jacques and Alden secured the canoe. By the time they were finished, Victoria was gone. Jacques spoke up. "I'm going to the gravesite. I won't be long, and I hope Mamman (Mama) will come back with me."

Jacques left Alden with the gear and silently disappeared on the trail. A short while later, he and Victoria reappeared. Alden had a blanket spread and their meager lunch set out. They sat down. In the quietness, they seemed to breathe a deep sigh together.

Victoria spoke first. "You can tell by the smell of the air that we are close to open water, maybe even salt water. It is good we have stopped, for your father would want us to be together before we begin our new adventures. I can feel his assuring presence near us even now."

Alden spoke up uncomfortably, "I saw an Osprey and an Eagle just a short time back. Those big birds are only found around open water for they find better fishing there."

Just then a large fish jumped only a few feet from shore. It slapped down on the surface with a loud clap that startled them.

"The fish reminds me," Victoria said, "of all of us – sort of fish out of water, searching for something, something new. We are each starting a new life. We need to grow whatever we do, together or apart. That is surely what your father would have wanted."

Jacques became uncomfortable with the tone of his mother's talk. *Whatever we do, together or apart,* echoed in his head. He missed his father now, for Marc would know exactly what to do. Jacques, now the man of the family, was not at all sure.

"What do you mean, Mother?" Jacques queried.

Victoria had gathered up the food and placed it back into the food satchel for storage. "Here," she said to Alden, "Put this in the canoe for us and leave Jacques and me alone for a bit."

Alden exchanged a puzzled look with Jacques, but gathered up the satchel and did as Victoria asked. Soon Jacques and his mother sat alone in silence listening to the wind and the song birds in the trees around them.

"You are a man now, son." She hesitated, searching for the right words. "I have decided to return to my family on the bayou. Bayou la Bateau was my home, and I have kin there who will help me start over. I loved your father deeply, and it will be hard to get past his death, but we must." She wiped her eyes with a cloth.

Jacques spoke up. "But what about…?"

Victoria cut him off with her raised hand.

"I am returning to the bayou and hope to find another underground rail crew, but not right away." She reached for Jacques' hand and pulled it to her face. She kissed it, and Jacques saw her tears. He was lost as to what to say or do.

"Tomorrow morning we are meeting a man at the point near the mouth of this river. His name is Alex Hoover, and he wants you to work for him."

Jacques started to speak…

"No! Just listen now. Alex works on a big boat, a steamer I think it's called. You have spoken of boats and sailing for a long time, and this is your chance. You're a quick learner. I've told Alex and his boss all about you. They were friends of your father's, and they expect you will be a large help to them. We will separate our gear tonight. You must be ready to join them at daylight."

Jacques was nearly breathless.

"Well, say something," Victoria chided him. "What? Cat got your tongue?" She smiled and laughed through her remaining tears.

Jacques moved close and hugged his mother. "Yes, I will make both you and father proud. I'm excited for such an opportunity, but I can't help but worry about you."

She pushed away slightly, "What? You don't think I can care for myself? Don't worry. You'd better make me proud, or I may have to come aboard that boat and straighten you out myself."

They both smiled, yet they were both unsettled with fears of what their new lives might hold.

"What about Alden?" Jacques asked.

Just then, as if on cue, Alden reappeared. "Okay for me to join the circle now?"

Jacques motioned him over.

"Alden is coming with me." Victoria said. "For one, I need his help with the canoe. Secondly, he can help me settle in. Then he can decide what's next for him."

"Would you like to come on the ship with me?" Jacques asked.

"I'm worried I couldn't handle the work," Alden replied holding up his injured hand. "I'm not sure."

Jacques nodded his understanding.

"But I bet there are lots of jobs you could do. You would be a huge help, especially with your knowledge of maps and navigation. Please think about coming on board. Then neither of us would be alone."

They smiled at each other as Victoria hurried them into the canoe. They only had a few hours of daylight to reach the point. The next day was going to be a big one!

Jacques did not sleep at all well that night. He was up before dawn, lit a fire, and started some coffee. The others then stirred, probably to the smell of his very strong coffee. As dawn lit the eastern sky, Jacques noticed a large shadow out on the bay. As it came closer, it was obviously a boat. It slowed, dropped anchor, and simply seemed to sit there for a while. Then he heard the sound of oars. A small row boat was making its way toward them. They put up the universal two-light signal to tell them all was clear.

The boat scraped the shore as it landed. Jacques, Alden, and Victoria hurried to the landing site as two men walked up on the shore. Neither was recognizable in the dim lantern light.

"Victoria?" the taller man asked.

"Alex, it is so good to see you." She stepped forward, shook his hand, and then they hugged.

"I was so shocked and saddened by Marc's death," he said as he held her hand softly. "How are you? I know it must be terribly hard."

She smiled and choked back a tear. "We're making do," is all she said.

Alex looked beyond Victoria and spied Jacques.

"Is this my new sailor?" He moved and shook Jacques' hand. "I am Captain Alex Hoover, and I would recognize you anywhere. You look like your father. You do not remember me, but I was on the ship years ago when you and your father visited my boss, Captain JW." He laughed, "But you were a bit smaller then!" Everyone smiled and appreciated the humor which broke some of the tension. "You have grown to be a strapping young man."

Jacques stood proudly and nodded. "Just passed my eighteenth birthday last month."

"I know your father would be proud of you," Captain Alex responded.

"A new day," Victoria said noticing the sun peeking over the eastern trees. Everyone looked east, paused, and contemplated the future, as they sipped their coffee.

"A new day for all of us," Victoria offered and lifted her cup in a toast.

"Here's to Marc," added Captain Alex, as he too lifted his cup.

All echoed, "Hear, Hear."

8

JACQUES THREW HIS bag aboard the steamer. He waved to his mother as Captain Alex steered the steamer, *Ole Miss,* out into the river. Jacques was so excited he forgot to be afraid, and that is the way his life was for the next six years. He worked with Captain Alex and learned about ships and their special role in the movement of fugitives. Captain Alex's admiration for Jacques' father, Marc, made his relationship to Jacques feel much more like a father/son relationship than one of a captain and crew. They traveled up and down that stretch of the Mississippi from where the Ohio enters at Cairo, Illinois, and back down toward New Orleans.

The trip for fugitive slaves from the Deep South was complicated and getting worse. The threat of war was all around. People in the North and the South were drawing lines and picking sides.

Now that Captain Walker had set up Captain Alex's ship to go north, movement of their ever expanding Cargo was faster. But with bounty hunters looking at every trail and ship with suspicion of being complicit in the illegal transport of fugitives, travel was always treacherous.

Even simple stops along the way for water were dangerous. All were suspect. Basic wood supply stops might mean searches, destruction of property, or physical harm. Jacques and Captain Alex had escaped many such encounters in their years together.

Captain Alex's task was to traffic Cargo north on the Mississippi River to its confluence with the Ohio. The Ohio River was important to the fugitive slave movement because, for hundreds of miles, it was the border between Slave States and Free States. Many a fugitive's goal was simply to make it across the Ohio River.

On a recent trip, Alex and Jacques had transported their human Cargo along with their regular cargo of southern cotton and molasses to Cairo, Illinois. The city was buzzing with business. . Some business was of fugitives coming and going. There was also much trade in common goods. Cairo was the gateway for many settlers going west into the newly opened territories. Jacques and Alex had stopped in Cairo, but were not able to leave their human Cargo there because of the threatening presence of bounty hunters.

Before they could move away from the dock, a mob of six heavily armed men stormed aboard demanding the release of the fugitive slaves. Captain Alex was a smooth talker. He let the men search at will, secure in the fact he was well prepared. His human Cargo was well hidden. After many minutes of searching, the men left, but not before one grabbed Jacques by the shirt, stuck his pistol under his chin, and threatened, "You sound like a Southern boy, and you's dark enough to be a Nigger, so's you watch your step or next you'll be steppin' off down South and be sold yo' self!"

After the men left, Jacques was still shaking from the threat. He had been fortunate to have escaped most of the violence in their work thus far. Maybe that was changing. He vowed he'd better learn how to defend himself, the Cargo, and the boat. Quickly Jacques helped push *Ole Miss* off, away from the dock and the angry men.

Not much later, Captain Alex and Jacques were transporting supplies to the developing cities on both sides of the Ohio River. They also picked up some fugitive Cargo and helped them cross to the north side of the river. That time there had been no problem or incident.

However, on downstream at their next stop near Cincinnati, there was a commotion on the dock as they approached. Men were shouting, torches flared, and guns waved about wildly. Suddenly a horse and buggy approached at a fast pace, nearly running into the group. The men scattered; the driver pulled up sharply. They all gasped, for it looked like the horse would surely slip on the boards and fall into the river. No one could see who was in the carriage, but two men ran up, one on each side. They were quickly handed something by the invisible driver in the buggy. If words were exchanged, none were heard. One man ran back to the noisy group. The other jumped the water gap, for the *Ole Miss* had not yet docked, and handed the note to Captain Alex. He took it, gave it a quick look, and quickly ordered 'reverse engines.' Jacques had been on deck and he guided Alex as they pulled out of the busy harbor and back into the river. They steamed away as fast as they could.

Jacques continued watching the activity on the dock. The person driving the buggy whirled it around and again drove it at the group still gathered. The mob separated again, in fear for their lives. The ragged group ran after the buggy as it headed back down the narrow road and away from the dock.

Alex took his crew downstream only a short distance and slowed near a point of rock jutting out from the bank about a hundred feet. The *Ole Miss* moved just past and dropped the rear anchor, allowing the current to pull it quickly in behind the point. Jacques moved to the wheelhouse and, as he entered to inquire what was happening, Capt. Alex pointed toward the shore.

There were two white flags flying, signaling it was safe to land.

"Lower the dingy and hurry to shore," he said to Jacques, waving him on his way.

Jacques and Mack moved into the dingy but they approached the landing cautiously. A darkly dressed person stepped out from the brush. In the dim light of evening, Jacques believed it was a woman. The person signaled for them to land.

When she dropped the hood from her cape, Jacques was stunned. She was indeed a woman, a very beautiful young woman. He stuttered, "Can, Can I, ah, help you, Ma'am?"

Their eyes met and they were attracted like the pull of a magnet. But there was no time for that. Quickly back on task, the women replied, "Ah, yes, I'm Darlene Babcock Coffin, Levi Coffin's daughter. Your fugitive Cargo can land safely here. I'm sorry for the untimely mix-up at the other dockage upstream."

With that, she stepped into the dingy, and they rowed back to the *Ole Miss.*

Alex was at the railing and helped Miss Coffin climb aboard. With some quick directions, the Cargo, a family of five and two separate women, were escorted from the bulkhead hiding space and ferried to the shore. It took two trips.

When done, Miss Coffin bid Alex adieu and lowered herself into the dingy. Jacques and Mack carefully transported the lady back to shore and helped her from the boat. As they stood there somewhat nervously, two wagons joined them and loaded their Cargo. The teams were turned, and exited quickly into the darkness. It was hard to see, but Jacques could just make out the outline of a lone horse and buggy which certainly belonged to Miss Coffin. How fearless she had been! How brave to risk everything to save the mission. He was in awe and truly smitten. He offered his hand, helped her to the buggy, and guided her into the seat. Their eyes met again.

"We've not been officially introduced," she said extending her hand to Jacques.

Jacques shyly removed his cap. "I am Jacques Bateau, first mate of Captain Alex."

"I am Darlene Babcock Coffin, as I told your captain. I am Levi Coffin's daughter."

"Very pleased to meet you, Ma'am. You must be very proud of your father. We all know of his hard work and sacrifice. He is an inspiration to us all. I've heard him called the 'President of the Underground Railroad.' It is wonderful that you work to make his dream a reality."

She smiled and let go of Jacques' hand. She took the reins and pulled the buggy from under the tree. Jacques stepped back out of the way.

"I do believe there are future plans to have your captain transport more fugitive Cargo this way. Do look me up again when you are in the Cincinnati area." With that she slapped the reins and the horse started off with a jump.

"I will," Jacques shouted, but surely he could not have been heard. *Oh, yes, I surely will,* he breathed under his breath.

Captain Alex moved east up the Ohio, as they'd been secretly directed by the area directors of the Underground Railroad. Not far up the river, Captain Alex pointed out where the Tennessee River joined from the south. One of the fugitive Cargo, emerged from the hidden bulkhead room behind the boiler, joined the crew, and told them the story of the song *Follow the Drinkin' Gourd* whose words are really directions for fugitives escaping Mississippi slavery. First, he told of the Tombigbee River that flows north through much of Mississippi. Then the song says to "see the two mountains and just beyond them is the Tennessee River and on to the Ohio. There, Peg-leg Pete would take them across the Ohio to freedom." Jacques was amazed at the important message in that simple song.

A short way past the Tennessee River and on the north side, Captain Alex saw the signal to pull in. It was too shallow to land. So, in the dark, the boat was anchored. Two skiffs came out to the boat. The crew hurriedly off-loaded their fifteen passengers onto the skiffs which quietly disappeared into the darkness of the shore. The Captain weighed anchor and quickly turned back west to pick up more regular cargo going south to a port near Memphis. To anyone else it appeared that *Ole Miss* was a normal steamer carrying cargo back and forth on the big river.

The village where the Cargo had been dropped was a settlement of freed black families in the southwest corner of Illinois. It was called *New Liberty*. The people of New Liberty, although free, were under constant threat from bounty hunters from the South and local pro-slavery advocates called copperheads. The citizens of Liberty continued to be faithful to the abolitionist cause, making Liberty a key station on the trail North. The symbolic name, New Liberty, meant a lot to Jacques. He took pride in his work and was constantly reminded that his was a noble effort.

Over their years together, Jacques and Captain Alex grew close. Jacques watched every detail of Captain Alex's work, asked many questions, and kept notes of the answers. They enjoyed each other's company and, after so many adventures, had grown to rely on each other. Still, they knew in the backs of their minds, they would one day part.

That day did arrive. While docked near Cairo, Illinois, Captain Alex called Jacques to the wheelhouse.

"Yes, sir? Did you call for me?" Jacques inquired. The ship was waiting for their next shipment, so all was quiet. Most of the crew had taken the opportunity to rest or go ashore for some 'refreshment.'

"Yes, Jacques. Come in and pull up a stool. I was organizing some of the maps and charts. We need to be well organized when we meet the next crew south of Shiloh next week."

Jacques was bit puzzled. He said nothing and started to help Captain Alex roll and sort maps. They had a special rack to store them in, and Jacques helped get them back into their correct places.

"Here, you will need this one the most, so keep it out on the top." Captain Alex handed Jacques a map, but hesitated when he saw the puzzled look on Jacques' face. "Oh, my young friend, I have gotten ahead of myself. Here, set this stuff aside and share some tea. I've just made a fresh pot."

Jacques complied, took his cup, sipped, and waited.

"Ah...I guess I don't know how to say this easily. You are well aware of Captain Walker's tribulations down in Florida and New Orleans. The result of all that is that JW is returning to Massachusetts, and he has asked me to return to New Orleans to take over his work there." Alex paused, sipped some tea, and waited for a reaction from his now First Mate, Jacques.

"You mentioned meeting another crew. Is *Ole Miss* going south with you? Why another crew? We have a crew. What about....?"

Jacques began to fire off questions like a repeating rifle. Captain Alex raised his hand to stop Jacques' mind from racing.

"Like I said, I don't know how to make this all make easy sense. What I am building up to is this. I am appointing you the captain of

Ole Miss. I am going back to the South with the new crew to continue Captain Walker's work on another ship." He paused again and looked Jacques square in the eye. "You are like a son to me, and I have been honored to be your teacher. Your father, Marc, would be very proud of the work you have done."

It took a couple days for Captain Alex's news to sink in. Jacques went from feeling excitement to fear, from being proud to humble. He was thrilled to honor the memory of his father. He would work harder still to continue to make him proud.

It took some time for arrangements to be cleared but, finally, the *Ole Miss* headed south toward the bayou, to the rendezvous with Captain Alex's new crew. Preparations for the transfer of leadership were made. Jacques was pleased to have the crew he had grown to trust choose to stay and work with him. He was especially happy when his closest friend, Mack, the engineer, came to assure Jacques of the crew's support.

The exchange of command occurred quickly. As was tradition, Captain Alex simply saluted the new Captain and left *Ole Miss* in Jacques' capable hands. No time for ceremonies. Work needed to be done, so Captain Jacques Bateau moved the ship out into the channel and steamed off.

A short distance up the river, Jacques pulled *Ole Miss* into a small cove and anchored. He had two tasks to accomplish. Earlier, he had sent a letter to his mother in New Orleans. Since he would soon be moving farther north, he wanted to see her, maybe for the last time. Now at anchor, he called two of his crew together, gave them the paint, and set them to work. Jacques did not hesitate for a minute in deciding what he would name the boat he now commanded. At the end of the day, Jacques and Mack lowered the dingy and paddled out to look at the bow. They sat smiling at each other. Jacques beamed as he saw the results of his men's work. His ship, formerly *Ole Miss*, would now be known as *L'Étoile Polaire*, The North Star.

Having to keep their movements secretive, the newly christened ship sailed off in the darkness to the rendezvous at Isle Polaire. Jacques and his crew proudly pulled into the dockage and tied up. Jacques jumped off the ship into the arms of his mother. They had so little time. Victoria had been dropped on the island by a Captain Walker steamer and was scheduled to be picked up in a short three hours, about dawn. They talked and shared memories. It was a good meeting, but a sad one. Too soon, it would be time for them to go back to their separate lives and work.

He and Victoria stood in silence. *Another parting,* he thought to himself. It had been over six years and a lot of experiences since he and his mother had buried his father's remains on Isle Polaire. Jacques was now in his twenties. He and his mother had come back to visit this little island only once, just before Jacques left to sail with Captain Alex. *Will this be our last visit?* Jacques' thoughts rattled in his head.

"A part of us will always be here, my son." Victoria looked off at the light starting to show in the eastern sky. "Our darkness is only temporary as we move ahead in our lives. Look at you! Your father would be so proud. You've become a captain, of your own ship, *L'Étoile Polaire*. You've mastered skills you never could have imagined back in the bayou with only our two canoes."

Jacques took his mother's hand in his, raised it to his lips, and kissed it. *She was so right, as always.*

In the years they had been apart, much had happened in Victoria's life. She had moved to New Orleans to continue her work transporting fugitive slaves. Many slaves were being sold south away from the Border

States where they might possibly escape. In the Deep South where Victoria lived, the slaves' work was even harder. The anticipated war had begun, and the raging conflict made it even worse. It was harder on the slaves forced to stay and harder to transport those trying to escape.

Jacques spoke up, "Mamman (mama), you have done well. I am so glad you and Burt are together. I was saddened to hear of Gloria's death. Our work is always rife with danger, as we both well know." They held each other and thought about Marc's death those many years ago. "Make sure Burt knows how much I appreciate him for the support he gave me after Father died. I feel like I owe him."

"I surely will, son. He thinks the world of you and mentions you often." Victoria smiled and laughed. "Do you remember the canoe paddle you and your father found? The one with the Indian symbols? It has continued to give your Spirit protection."

"Yes, I believe it does." Jacques walked over nearer to his father's grave and removed a clump of branches, revealing a surprise for his mother. She gasped.

"Yes," Jacques explained. "I placed this paddle here soon after we parted, when I went on board ship with Captain Alex. I feel its Spirit mingles with Father's good spirit, protecting us both. Don't you agree?"

Victoria hugged her son as tears dotted her face. She dabbed her eyes with the tail of her long sleeved shirt.

"As you have grown older, you not only resemble your father more and more physically, but you've become wise like him as well. Like you, he believed that our work, though dangerous, was blessed by the Good Spirits. That is why he, and all of us, are pledged to give even our lives, as he has done. You will do well, my son. May Marc's good spirit lead you in your new adventures in the North. Where will you go first?" she asked.

They sat on a rock near the steamer's dockage. Jacques began, "You know that since Captain Walker was arrested, branded, and jailed, our whole organization has been in turmoil. The authorities branded him with 'SS' for 'Slave Stealer.'" However, our leaders choose to call the brand 'Slave Salvation' because they feel his sacrifice will convert more people to our cause. JW is not well after his jail ordeal and is returning to Massachusetts. Captain Alex has been asked to replace JW and continue his work around New Orleans on over to Florida. In turn, Captain Alex has been grooming me to take over his work with his steamer." He motioned toward the moored ship, saying, "It's not much, but it will prove very helpful. We are re-positioning ourselves farther north."

"Near the Ohio?" his mother asked.

"Farther north yet, Mamman. We will be going to Chicago soon. We need to use lesser known routes North by utilizing this ship and the many navigable rivers on the west shore of this new territory, Michigan."

"Michigan? But it is so cold up there!"

"Yes," Jacques laughed. "I guess my Southern blood will have to get thicker!" They both smiled. Jacques continued. "I'm excited, and I have a new mate to work with. We met briefly during our trip to Cairo and Liberty last month. His name is Arch McGuire, and he, like me has French Canadian-Indian heritage. He has lived and worked in the area from Canada in the North to the Ohio River. He will be a valuable resource, for he is familiar with all those many streams I told you about. That gives us access to many alternative routes when and if we get harassed or discovered on a particular trail. There are already many well-placed friends, Quakers and Oberlin abolitionists, anxious to help move the fugitive slaves. Arch, my crew, and I are excited to be recruited to help along the way with this old steamer. It is a bit small for

Lake Michigan, but it will do fine up and down the coast and in or out of those smaller inlet rivers."

Victoria gazed at the ship. "*L'Étoile Polaire*," she said out loud. "How I remember your father saying so often '*N'oublie pas, L'Étoile Polaire*' (Don't forget the North Star) when he would leave on a mission. It will guide you well, my son. But look, the sky is brightening. We should be gone by sun up."

They hurried to erase their tracks so no one could possibly trace their whereabouts and boarded Jacques' ship. He took the controls and maneuvered out around the shoals near the island. Soon they neared the lee side of the island and saw the two-light signal. They acknowledged the signal, and, as they slowed, a four-oared skiff met them. Only time for one quick hug, and Victoria was deftly over the side and gone.

Jacques moved *L'Étoile Polaire* away quickly so as not to draw attention. As he rounded the north end of the next island, the sun's bright rays greeted him. Jacques smiled at the good sign.

The sun was rising on a new day for all.

Fearful they might not again meet,

But faithful of their lives' guiding spirit heeded.

All - mother, child, and *L'Étoile Polaire* -

Will be blessedly led wherever it's needed.

9

ARCH MCGUIRE, THE new first mate, clamored on board the *L'Étoile Polaire* as it briefly stopped near Liberty, Illinois. They smiled and greeted each other warmly as Jacques moved the steamer back out into the river. Jacques pointed out their destination on the map dimly lit by the swaying lantern. They would be stopping farther up the Ohio River, near where the Wabashoo River flowed in from the north. There they were to take on a cargo of general goods and tools. These were to be delivered to two different outposts as they traversed north on the Illinois River to Chicago. This area was also a common spot for fugitives crossing the Ohio. Jacques noticed a village named New Haven. He smiled as he knew it was surely a new haven for those on the road to freedom.

Jacques introduced Arch to the rest of the crew, including his closest friend and ally, Mack, the engineer. Jacques showed Arch around the ship, which was actually a small schooner, especially when compared to many others used on the Great Lakes. *L'Étoile Polaire* measured only 74' stem to stern and drafted only six and a half feet. Arch admired the rigging work Jacques had accomplished. He and Mack had added two short masts holding three medium sized sails of about 20'x20' giving them a wind power advantage in addition to the regular steam engine propeller.

"Why the rigging?" Arch inquired.

"Mostly the idea was to have some extra power on Lake Michigan, for this is a fairly small ship," Jacques replied. "However, I've enjoyed another advantage I'd not expected."

Jacques motioned Arch out on the deck outside the wheel house.

"Listen," Jacques cocked his hand to his ear.

"Listen to what? I don't hear anything," Arch replied.

"That's it exactly!" They moved back inside to mind the steering. "You see, we're now moving nearly silent with no sound of the engine."

Arch smiled and nodded, "Oh, yes! I get it. The key advantage will be silence. The sails allow us to move more quietly in and out of the numerous small ports we'll visit up the western coast of Michigan."

"Yes, and we still have the steam capacity, so together we've more speed and more options, especially if there is no wind and we need to get away fast or hurry to a new destination." They both smiled at the thoughts of their up-coming travels.

"I'm really looking forward to seeing this work when we arrive up North," Arch told Jacques.

"You go on below and catch some sleep. Mack and I can keep us on course for a while. You come spare us at daylight."

Arch yawned in agreement and disappeared out of the wheel house. Clattering footsteps could be heard as he descended the metal ladder, and Jacques was again in silence.

Jacques moved the small oil lamp over closer to his map table. Actually it was less of a table, more like a wide board hinged to the wall so it could be dropped down as a table, then pulled up out of the way when not needed. It would be hooked to the ceiling to give enough room for at least two or more persons to be in the wheel room at one time. It was always very tight in that vital, busy space.

The river map was easy enough. Mostly they were trying to stay away from the shoals and sand bars. Jacques was heading east against the current, so he kept the sails up and moved along slowly. No other craft was visible on the river. He knew he was nearing the pickup site, so he pulled the ship closer to shore and dropped anchor to wait for daylight. He noticed the eastern sky getting light, so it wouldn't be long. He took out his journal and logged in his progress.

Jacques paused as he entered, *Picked up Arch McGuire at New Liberty. Looking forward to his assistance. Quiet guy. Will fit in well.* Jacques recalled their first meetings and Captain Alex's encouragement. Alex had assured Jacques that the two of them, he and Arch, would be a good combination. *Hope he was right,* Jacques said to no one.

Soon after daylight, Arch appeared with cups of steaming coffee.

"I hope this is drinkable," he said. "I'm no cook. I just rummaged around and found what I think is coffee. Try it!"

"Steaming hot always hits the spot!" Jacques chimed in with his best wit. "Say, Arch, Captain Alex referred to you as Tomahawk McGuire. Is that a nickname or a bad Indian stereotype?"

Arch looked deeply at Jacques over his steaming coffee. Jacques hoped he had not stepped over a boundary with this new friend. Neither men said anything for some time. Finally, Arch responded. "Maybe I'll tell you about it later."

That was all that was said. The two men both understood that, sometimes, silence was a good way to communicate.

They made good progress through the night. Now they powered up and moved out into the river. They were approaching their destination. Jacques pointed out their position on the map. Arch was familiar with the area and nodded in agreement. With the daylight came a cloudy day with a hint of drizzle.

"This is good," Arch offered. "These cool rains tend to keep those Southern bounty hunters with their thin blood pretty much under cover and out of our hair."

Within a short time they were tied up at wharf number four and directed to an office. The sign over the door read, 'Northern Freight.' Neither men knew if that was the company name or where freight going north was being dispensed. All they knew was it was a safe place to do business. The office was small. Even though there were only two staffers, it seemed busy and crowded. Papers, directions, and maps were discussed, exchanged, and signed. All were stuffed into a large oiled envelope.

The agent, Mr. Dryfus, was all business as he yelled out the door for his helper. "Here, Jackson," and handed him the load list. "Get these goods loaded on that steamer at Dock #4. Quickly, mind you. There's a storm comin' and these men want to be on their way west."

All was soon accomplished. Arch and Mack directed the dockhands where to put the crates, which were then fastened and braced solidly. Arch and Mack knew to be careful not to cover or impair access to the bulkhead storage. When everything was loaded, Capt. Jacques double checked the lists and the load-order, signed the lading bills, shook hands with Mr. Dryfus, and reboarded the *L'Étoile Polaire*. Like its name, it was time to head north toward the new adventure.

One of the dockhands inquired to Arch about the ship's name. "I don't understand the name," he said.

"It's French," Arch replied and pronounced it with a wonderful French accent.

"What's it mean?" the man asked.

"North Star! That star is a sailor's delight and has directed many a trip."

The man quieted his voice and leaned closer to Arch.

"And it has led many other Cargo away from the hell down South to the freedom of Canada. Listen, watch for the Northern Freight sign on up north. It will always be a safe place for your Cargo." He smiled, winked, patted Arch's shoulder, and was gone.

Arch paused there amazed, for in this work he never knew who were friends or foes. He looked at the Northern Freight sign, looked at their ship, looked up to some heaven far away, and muttered under his breath, "Great Spirit, North Star Spirit, guide us safely on this trip." He crossed himself out of habit and called to Jacques, "All lines off, all clear."

Jacques had the steam up. Arch and Mack jumped aboard as the ship eased away from the dock. Arch caught the eye of the man he'd just chatted with, and they exchanged a quiet smile and a tip of the hat.

Moving on downstream was going well. Mack had appeared from below deck with some much-needed food for sustenance. Knowing what was ahead, they'd best eat while they could. They moved the ship around the lee side of a small island. The river chart noted there was depth enough, and they anchored.

"We best get some rest," Jacques reminded the crew. "There will be lots of work later tonight." They agreed and moved off on their own.

Jacques bunked in the wheel house, so he pulled out a blanket and small pillow from a lower cabinet. As he settled, he thought of his mother and Burt. He was truly happy for them. *How life and fate...,* he paused, wondering if he believed in fate… better said, *how life moves on*. He knew his mother had loved his father. But she, too, was moving on, as Marc would have wished. She had married Burt. Jacques smiled, for, beyond his father, there was no one he loved and admired more than Burt.

He threw off his cover and reached for his writing material. *I think I'll write a note to them and post it later when we stop.* He quickly penned a letter and sealed it. His mind drifted. *Should I write another note?*

When talking to his mother some months back, Jacques had not shared every detail of what had happened in the ensuing years. He sat back, letting the waves rock his memory; he dozed, or maybe he dreamed. Or was he just remembering one of the tenderest moments of his recent years working with the Underground Railroad?

Darlene Babcock Coffin, he said to himself. Where might she be now? He was about twenty and she was about eighteen years old when they first met near Cincinnati. He recalled the incident very well. He was First Mate for Captain Alex and they were sailing the Ohio River. Jacques then dropped off into a deep reverie and time passed.

Suddenly, the *L'Étoile Polaire* rocked hard and Jacques came back to life in the present time. "Wow, that must have been over four years ago." Smiling, he tried to remember and recount the time as he lay there dreaming.

At two other times, he had visited the Cincinnati area with Captain Alex. On one trip, Alex had to go upstream farther, but he had dropped Jacques off in Cincinnati. Jacques had spent the whole day touring the city with Darlene. She showed him the settlements that were divided by hills they called mountains. The nearest one to the river was Mt.

Auburn. She pointed to her family's home sitting prominently on the top very visible to all.

"It's a bit of a beacon of hope to those who arrive on the opposite shore. They see Papa's house and know they've nearly arrived to safety." Darlene was a wonderful companion. It was the first day Jacques could recall relaxing in many years.

The day sped by too quickly and, as evening neared, Jacques and Darlene approached the dockage just as the *L'Étoile Polaire* was pulling in.

Alex yelled, "No time to dally. We're being followed."

Jacques nervously took Darlene's hand. Quickly, he simply kissed her hand and ran for the boat. As he cleared the rail, he saw her wave. That was the last he'd seen her.

But why did I suddenly think of her tonight? He wondered about the possibility of seeing her again. *Oh, well. At least I can write.* He could pen a note, *but where should I send it?*

Jacques was now fully awake as he finished his writing. The setting sun illuminated his wheelhouse. He stowed his pillow and blanket and went out to roust the others. As he stepped out, he was pleasantly surprised to see every one sitting around chatting with cups of coffee and some cold food for a meager meal.

"Yo, Captain," Mack called. "Did you have good dreams?"

Jacques smiled, nodded, and turned back to the wheelhouse. He thought to himself, *Oh, yes. I certainly did. If they only knew!*

10

Jacques posted two letters at the next stop. *Who knows? Maybe she'll remember me after this long absence. No time to worry about it now.* Like always, he, Mack, and Arch had a big job ahead.

For the next several years, Jacques and his crew worked up and down the Ohio River. Since the Civil War had been declared, fugitives were trying to leave the South in droves. Oddly, the Underground Railroad never handled large groups, but one by one, or one family by one family, they risked life and limb to travel to safety of the North. All was not perfect, for even in the no-slave states, bounty hunters were everywhere. Their work had been legalized by the passage of the Fugitive Slave Act back in 1850. Different states handled it differently, but danger prevailed for any fugitives until they could make it to Canada. Negro settlements were growing in Ontario. Some famous people like Harriet Tubman reportedly made dozens of trips in and out of the South leading slaves to Canada.

The inevitable war had commenced several years earlier. Jacques and his crew were lucky to stay clear of fighting, but there was increasing traffic on the river. There were many supply ships going back and forth. It was a struggle to keep up their own work and to stay out of the way of both the military and the slave catchers.

Jacques, Arch, Mack, and the rest of the crew worked hard practicing maneuvering their boat in and out of small ports and handling regular cargo that was their cover for the important work of helping their fugitive Cargo on their way to safe haven in Canada. The work kept them busy, and they grew very close as a team.

Not all their work was cheery and happy. Jacques still had nightmares about the night they rescued a man hanging onto a sinking rowboat. After dragging him aboard, he wept inconsolably, for he had lost his whole family. They had tried to cross at the same time together in a small boat. His wife and mother-in-law plus five small children were all swept away when the boat was capsized by the wake of a large paddle boat that surely did not see them. The wave had just been too much! After they capsized, several tried to hold onto each other, but one by one, they slipped away. The father sobbed and sobbed for his loss. Later that night, the man tried to jump overboard, wanting to drown with his family. He was restrained and pulled back aboard. One of Jacques' nightmares was of himself running around searching for that man. Jacques often wondered what ever happened to him after they left him off on the Ohio side of the river in the hands of some abolitionist friends.

Jacques was excited to have received new orders when he picked up mail at their last stop in Liberty, Illinois. It was time to take their ship and crew on to their new work in the North.

"How far north?" one of the crew, Jonathan, asked Captain Jacques.

"All the way into Lake Michigan. Yes, it will be colder, so better get ready." Jacques assured the crew they would be well. Some were excited, some were cautious, but most knew this was what they had trained to do. This new assignment was what they had been preparing for these past years. They were ready.

They traveled west on the Ohio, maybe for the last time. As they approached Cairo, Illinois, they reviewed their directions and soon located the Northern Freight warehouse along the docks. They were quickly unloaded, pulled away, and headed north. They only stopped once for fuel. Wood was more plentiful in this part of the country, with fewer inhabitants and fewer steamers in need of it.

Their next port of call was up river to where the Illinois River emptied into the Mississippi. The Illinois River would be their road to Chicago. The last of the outpost supplies on board were unloaded at a small place called Freight Junction. *An apt name,* Jacques thought. They were running high and light with no freight. Because of that, they made exceptionally good time.

They traveled up the Illinois River to the mouth of the Kankakee River. Arch, who knew the area because he had grown up in the vicinity, pulled out the map and motioned for Jacques to look on.

"We are here," he pointed. "The Native community has known of this alternate route around the Chicago area for years. The early French fur traders and explorers like LaSalle and Cavalier used this route. That must have been well over a century ago.'"

Jacques was impressed and encouraged by Arch's great knowledge of the many inland waterways.

Pointing out the spot on his map so Jacques would see, Arch went on, "We go up the Kankakee for many miles, to about here. From there it is a short portage of only two or three miles over the hill to what is called The Great Bend. That large bend is in the river listed on the map as the St. Joe River, but we Indians called it *The Great Ma-hab-ee*, meaning *Great Fishing River*. The point is that from this spot, the river flows nearly directly north to empty into Lake Michigan at the St. Joe settlement. At that big river bend, the river has come straight from the east. That part of the river has been a helpful alternative route when moving fugitives toward Canada through Detroit. Did you know the settlement you call St. Joe is the second oldest settlement in Michigan? There have been four flags flying over it through the years. First, there was the French, then the British, then the Spanish for a short time in 1781, and finally, the United States' flag since shortly after the Revolution. Now St. Joe is part of Michigan, one of the newest states of the Old Northwest Territory."

Jacques stared and listened intently as Arch demonstrated a part of himself Jacques had not seen before. He understood how important the route was to their work, but more so, he was in awe of Arch's mastery of the area.

"Now you can see how a little knowledge of geography is helpful in our work." Arch paused to decide what else he should show Jacques on the map.

"Yes, there are several other rivers, as you can see, that flow generally across Michigan nearly east to west. There's one here called 'the Grand' and one here called the Musk-ke-gone. Some of these also work as alternatives to move Cargo safely to Canada. Still other rivers serve to transport Cargo to remote lumber camps where they may find jobs. Others help us get to rivers that flow east into Lake Huron and on to Freedom."

"Yes," Jacques spoke up, "but Freedom is a long way across Lake Huron unless we go up the west side of the state towards the Michilimackinac area. The waterways all join together to make our task successful. I know we're going to see all those rivers and ports before this adventure is over."

Arch chuckled and again moved to the map, "Where this river flows into Lake Huron at Chewegon, it is just up the coast to our goal, Freedom." Jacques did not understand, for he believed the only real 'freedom' was the Cargo's arrival in Canada.

"See here," Arch pointed, "is a small community of free Negros and fugitive slaves. They have named their town 'Freedom.' So, we are on our way to Freedom."

Jacques and Arch laughed together. How ironic it was there was a town of 'Freedom.' They were both reminded of other towns they had visited with similar histories, towns such as New Liberty, Illinois, or New Haven, Indiana along the Ohio River. They both felt a part of a truly important undertaking..

It took Jacques, Mack, and Arch several weeks to make the journey to the Chicago area. The Illinois was navigable because of a series of locks and canals. At each, it meant a slowdown; there were inspections and fees. It was good they were riding empty and floating high, for their draft depth was minimal.

One evening they were stopped along one of the canals. They had gone onto the bank, lit a fire, and cooked their dinner of fresh pheasant. Arch, being part Indian, proved extremely useful for his hunting ability. Leave it to an Indian to be more accurate with a gun than an old river rat like Jacques from the bayou.

Mack and the remainder of the crew had gone back on board to get some sleep. Jacques yawned dreamily.

"You got any family, Arch? You've never spoke of any kin."

Arch picked at the coals in the fire, randomly stirring, seeming to ignore the question. Jacques was glad to let it drop; he'd come to respect Arch for his long, strong silences. Suddenly, Arch spoke. "My wife and I were only together for less than a year."

Jacques sat up in piqued interest. Then more silence. Jacques put a couple more pieces of wood on the fire. They were quite green, but the smoke helped keep the pesky mosquitos away.

Arch continued, "We were on the trail with two fugitives going to a station near Detroit. We natives were usually not suspect for some reason, and we usually got past most inspectors. That night, the fugitives were hiding in a wagon full of hay that we were hauling. It was dark, of course, when we heard noises ahead. There was loud talk, bad singing, and what sounded like drunk men. So I pulled off the road to hide, hoping they'd pass us in the darkness."

"There were three men on horseback. They continued to talk and sing loudly. When they came near our hiding place, one of the men got off his horse. Actually, I think he fell off because he was so drunk. He stumbled over toward us, I imagine to relieve himself. He didn't see us, but about then he yelled something to one of his companions, and that spooked my horse. The man drew his gun and fired into the darkness. I quickly pulled my gun and fired back, slapped my horse, and tore away."

Arch was silent again for some time. Jacques waited on his friend.

"You okay?" Jacques finally asked.

"She must have died instantly. One random shot by a drunk man who couldn't have hit a tree at ten paces in his stupor. We drove away very fast to get away from them, and I thought my wife, her name was Bright, was hiding behind me in fear. But when I stopped the wagon, I could see she was dead, shot in the head. Why not me? Why? Why? Why? That's all I ask, over and over."

Jacques and Arch sat there in silence for a long while. Finally, Arch rose. "Goin' for a walk." That's all he said.

The next morning, Arch had not returned. A team of mules arrived to pull the boat through a shallow wooded section where it could not go forward under its own power. Jacques asked the other men if they'd seen Arch; he even walked on down the trail in the direction Arch had gone. But there was no sign of him.

They had to move on, so they did. They traveled all morning and arrived at the next lock. Their boat entered, the gates closed, and the boat was lowered to the next level. The next stretch of the river was deep enough, and they prepared to proceed under their own power. Jacques stalled and stalled. But, finally, they had to move out. As he shouted to the men to throw off the lines, he looked at the front line and smiled.

Arch unhooked the line, threw it aboard, and yelled to Captain Jacques, "Bow line gone!" He jumped the water gap as they pulled away from the shore. Jacques never pushed Arch to share again. Their work just went on. They were a good team.

They were much alike. They were both part French Canadian. Jacques' father was southern Louisiana French, but was born in Quebec. Arch was also born in Quebec, to a French Canadian mother and an Indian father. The North and the South met on a ship in the middle of a river in the middle of the country. They were both deeply committed to their passion for freedom; each carried his own losses. Maybe the pain they shared was a bond they shared as well.

Their closeness would reward them over and over. They knew the Great Spirit was always nearby.

⎯⎯⎯

ON TO LAKE MICHIGAN

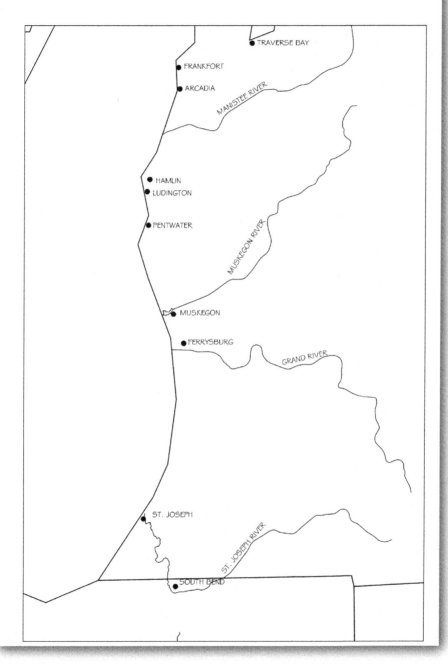

TRAVERSE BAY

FRANKFORT

ARCADIA

MANISTEE RIVER

HAMLIN

LUDINGTON

PENTWATER

MUSKEGON RIVER

MUSKEGON

FERRYSBURG

GRAND RIVER

ST. JOSEPH

ST. JOSEPH RIVER

SOUTH BEND

11

JACQUES AND ARCH found their way to Chicago and to their assigned dockage. They were nervous in their new environment. Everything was different and everything about Jacques set him apart. Everywhere he went, people seemed to wonder with their eyes. 'Who is he?' 'What is he up to?' First, Jacques' accent was different. He couldn't erase his Southern heritage, even if he had worked in the north for most of his life. His crew was also a mix: Arch, with his brimmed hat with one feather, and Mack, with his build and full beard, looking more like a bear from his Kentucky Appalachian roots than a sailor. The others, too, were a motley collection, loyal to the death to their Captain and to their mission.

And what about that ship? Was it a steamer or a schooner? Or both? A seventy foot steamer with two short masts was not a regular sight. Albeit the schooner ruled the traffic on Lake Michigan in this age of lumber, they came in all sizes from small ones at 50' to large 150' ones with three masts and twenty-four sails. Mostly folks were curious about the name. *What is 'L'Étoile Polaire' supposed to mean? Were these men from another country?* The questions were many and created a suspicious tone everywhere they were.

They were all together in a smoky, dark roadhouse just up the road from the river dockage where the boat was moored. Food was ordered, moderate drink was allowed, but no excess or the guilty party would answer to Captain Jacques. No-one ever chose that alternative. They talked quietly, enjoying each other's company and a bit of rest from their constant on-the-go lifestyle. The boat was loaded and on the morrow, they'd head north.

A man with an unusual beard approached their table. Not sure of who was who, he asked, sort of to everyone, "Could I speak with Captain Bateau?"

The men looked at Jacques, and he motioned them to move away to another area of the room. Jacques stood and motioned for the visitor to sit with him.

"My name is Jacques Bateau," he said, extending his hand.

"Mine is Peter Schmidt. I'm told you might help me in my need to transport some valuable Cargo? Would ye be able?"

His use of words and his beard revealed his Quaker background. Jacques knew that, in the movement, many contacts throughout Pennsylvania, Ohio, Indiana, and Illinois were Quakers. Their religion was one of peace with strong abolitionist roots. They continued their work fearlessly and passionately.

Mr. Schmidt explained he and his people seemed to be highly suspect by a local band of bounty hunters. He was sure they were keeping close tabs on him. In fact, he warned Jacques, he had probably been followed to this area. However, arriving in the dark and coming this far north, he hoped he had thrown them off, at least temporarily. For that reason, he was traveling alone. Jacques and Peter discussed Peter's needs and made plans. It was decided that a diversionary move would help confuse the bounty hunters and better protect the fugitive Cargo.

Jacques called Arch over to the table. After quick introductions and an outline of the plan, Arch excused himself and left by a back entrance. Mr. Schmidt stayed a while so as to not raise suspicion. Then he walked to the front, paid his tab, and bid farewell.

Arch met up with Peter at a prearranged location. They discussed plans, maps, contacts, and other details. Wasting no time, they parted with a hearty handshake. But first, Peter stopped Arch and whispered his blessing. "Be blessed and travel well with the Great Spirit to guide and protect thee."

Arch smiled, crossed himself, and replied, "And the same for thee, sir."

After the two men left the roadhouse, Jacques returned to sit with his crew. Conversation was ebbing and, one by one, the crew returned to the ship to get ready for their sun-rise departure. All was well. No one seemed to be concerned about Arch's absence. Only Jacques knew Arch had received instructions to lead a group up the Kankakee River to the Big Bend and on to Lake Michigan by way of the St. Joe River. They would meet at the settlement near the mouth of the St. Joe River a couple of days hence.

Jacques smiled as he lay down that night thinking of the new mission. He was certainly blessed to have Arch and his knowledge of alternative trails and rivers. Coincidentally, Jacques remembered that he and Arch had just discussed such a route weeks earlier as they were approaching Chicago.

The necessary diversion was accomplished by having one of Peter Schmidt's crew drive a covered wagon and meet Jacques at the roadhouse just before daybreak. Four darkly clad people moved from the building to the wagon so as to appear to be the Cargo they were transporting northward. As expected, the wagon was followed. The bounty hunters were surprised when about twenty miles beyond the roadhouse, the wagon stopped at a farm. Having shed their dark clothes, and with the cover of the wagon folded back, the four smiling men unloaded with their harvesting tools ready to help the farmer harvest his crop. The diversion had gone off without a hitch.

During the night, there was had been action at the dock. Peter and his buggy appeared at Jacques' boat. Peter quickly unloaded four persons, two adults and two children, one in his mother's arms. Jacques quickly escorted them to his boat and hid them among the shipping boxes. All was quiet, food was shared, and much-needed rest was at hand.

Peter was well practiced at this deception. There was yet another group of Peter's that Arch was helping. Peter had split up his people and his Cargo to ensure the safety of both groups. Jacques had a wonderful feeling realizing he was a part, albeit a small part, of such a large, complicated system to move fugitives to safety. Freedom was a wonderful goal.

The dawning morning found a busy hustle and bustle on the dock as last details were dealt with. Some new cargo was loaded. Everyone was anxious, for several of the crates were large and cumbersome. Everyone gasped as one large crate tipped precariously toward the dark waters between the old dock and the ship's deck. One old dock hand was quick enough to redirect the crate away from the double catastrophe of losing the cargo into the river or having it drop back onto the wharf, possibly crushing someone.

It was a normal scene at Wharf #14, which was quite far down river and away from the bustling docks of the Chicago Harbor. Throughout the day, Jacques' crew worked efficiently to finish loading their cargo while a strange man stood in the shadows of the building. He held the reins of his team and waited. The horses were impatient and shook their harnesses. The bells had been removed so they did not make any noise to draw attention. The man spoke quietly and comforted them.

He, too, had nervously watched as the carton faltered. After that carton was steadied and loaded, there were two more similar crates to load. The next one faltered also as a small swell caused the ship to suddenly rise and settle. It tipped first toward the water, then settled back toward the dock. There were no panicky shouts of direction or alarm, for no one wanted to attract attention to the loading. Everything had to appear normal. The crew hurried to steady each crate. However, unexpectedly, one of the ropes went slack, and one carton turned on its corner and came crashing down on the wharf.

Everyone gasped, especially the shadowed stranger with his wagon and team. He nervously took two steps toward the dock, but stayed hidden in the shadows. Jacques' glance went from crewman to crewman, and he looked nervously up the hill to where the stranger stood unnoticed by everyone except Jacques.

Jacques thoughts raced. *What if... What if that crate is the one holding our Special Cargo?*

The crate hit the wharf and everyone scattered. No one was hurt. It landed on its corner and split wide open upon impact. All hands rushed forward. They were relieved no dockhand had been injured. But others wondered *What if...?* Then, out of the broken box tumbled two large metal gears made for a grinder at some distant mill.

Jacques showed just the hint of relief at seeing the gears clunk onto the dock. One even rolled up against the rickety wharf building, cracking the wall board where it stopped.

The crew exchanged glances of relief. Thank goodness the carton contained regular cargo not fugitive Cargo. The stranger put the reins over the team's heads, mounted the wagon seat, and spoke to the team. The horses responded quickly, turned sharply, and disappeared from sight. All hurried to retrieve the cargo. Jacques and his crew quickly repaired the crate, repacked the cargo, and this time successfully got it loaded.

The journey up Lake Michigan could finally get underway. All were glad: Jacques, the crew, and especially the special Cargo. It was always risky travel; they had done it before, but not in this waterway. There was more Cargo expected at the next port. They could afford no further delay.

As Jacques eased the ship from the wharf, he began to relax. The Quaker gentleman, Mr. Peter Schmidt, whom he had just met, had explained to him about this practice of 'shipping Cargo' along with other crates. Peter explained he had talked to one of his family contacts in Pennsylvania where he'd first heard of the idea. It appears a lumberman in Northwest Pennsylvania was shipping most of his lumber by train north through New York and on to Canada. The man was an abolitionist and hit upon the idea of constructing his lumber cars with hidden Cargo spaces. By that method he was able to move more people more quickly than by the land routes they had used for years.

Peter explained that several of his carpenter friends came up with the idea of using the crates on ships. They could be combined with any other method of shipping. Unfortunately, the Midwest did not have as many railroads as there were in the East. So the boats became more important. That was probably what Captain Walker had learned and why he and his crew had moved to the Midwest to increase the shipping traffic in Lake Michigan. It was a natural. There were many schooners and steamers in the area, one more would fit in and not be noticed.

Getting his mind back on his work, Jacques was nervous. This was his first effort with the crate system. The freight was stored securely in his ship, and the special crates were packed so they were accessible to provide food and water. Before he left, Peter had chided him, 'What is there to worry about?'

Plenty, Jacques wanted to answer.

The ship slowly moved past larger vessels and warehouses on toward Lake Michigan. There was only one more obstacle. They had to clear the inspection area for the Port of Chicago. They were in line behind two other vessels, and everyone's nerves were on edge. Mack was in charge of the deck and the hold. As they neared the mooring, Jacques met Mack's eye. Mack gave a thumbs up and grinned. *I'm really thankful Mack is always so positive,* Jacques thought.

Thump, Thump! Two inspectors jumped on board. "Your papers, sir? And what is your destination?"

Mack handed the shorter man the formal packet. The taller man wandered and snooped around. Jacques came out of the wheel house and called to the visitors, "Good day, gentlemen. Welcome aboard the *L'Étoile Polaire.*"

"The what?" the taller man asked.

"The North Star; it's French, dummy. Ain't you had no schooling?" the shorter man shot back at his partner, laughing. He quickly examined the papers. After a few minutes, he seemed satisfied and handed them back to Mack.

"Oh, Captain, I see you're on your way north. Stopping in St. Joe seems a bit odd, if your cargo is being sent to Ferrysburg."

"Yes, sir, it is a courtesy stop," Jacques quickly replied. "One of my crew has family in the area and is taking leave for a time. We'll pick him up on the return trip in a couple days."

"Nice of you, Captain. Now on with the business at hand. Where is the ladder to the hold?"

Mack directed both men to the aft hatch. The shorter one looked down, and he motioned for the taller one to go and check it out. As he descended, another member of the crew assisted at the bottom to ensure he didn't slip. As usual, the floors and bilge of the ship were wet. This area was closest to the steamer's engine, so it also was noisy and hot.

The tall man searched briefly, then exclaimed something to the crewman which he could not hear. However, it was easy to read lips, *"It's too damn hot down here for me!"* He took out his handkerchief, wiped his brow, and proceeded to climb the ladder back to the deck.

"All seems in order, Captain," the lead man said. He scribbled his signature on the shipping sheet, waved, and prepared to depart. Mack attempted to assist both of them to the dock, but the taller man slapped away the hand that was offered to steady him as the boat rose and fell in the swells. Fortunately, both inspectors were able to disembark without incident.

Mack undid the lines, jumped the water gap, and pushed *L' Étoile Polaire* away from the dock with a pike pole. They waved and quietly let out a sweaty sigh of relief.

12

I T WAS DARK on Lake Michigan and the wind calmed. All noticed that the stars were out and the Big Dipper was clearly visible. Everyone relaxed and had some food. Night watches were scheduled.

Mack was on first watch and stood at the railing of the wheelhouse with Jacques.

"All seems good tonight," Jacques observed to Mack or no one.

Mack acknowledged with a quiet, "Ya," and then commented, "All seems good except we don't know where Arch is."

Jacques didn't directly answer Mack's backward question about his friend and first mate Arch.

"N'oublie pas, L'Étoile Polaire" is what my father always said. 'Just remember the North Star.' This work was like a religion to him, and he deeply believed the Great Spirit was guiding him in it. Arch believes the same, and he'll be guided."

There was a long lull in their conversation.

Then Jacques spoke again. "I remember my father would look up at those stars and start to sing. His favorite liberation song was 'Follow the Drinkin' Gourd,' about following that same Big Dipper we see to help people get to freedom. With that guiding them, they would always be 'in sight of freedom.' His second favorite was 'Bound for Glory,' which again was a guide and an inspiration for all in this work."

Jacques straightened and turned to his friend. In the dim light he sensed a look of worry on Mack's face.

"Remember," Jacques said, "Arch will see the same promise in the stars tonight that we do. He'll meet us soon. We'll pick him up, along with more valuable Cargo."

Jacques gave a deep sigh and lingered in his reflective mood. He had not reminisced about his father for a long time. His mind slipped back briefly to the bayou and his younger days. He missed his father deeply. Jacques took pleasure knowing he was carrying on the noble work his father had so diligently and passionately taught him.

Nautically speaking, the distance from Chicago to St. Joe was about fifty to sixty miles due east. With a good west wind, it would take about five hours. If they used steam power, they risked burning all their fuel, and it would still be about the same travel time. They were a bit behind schedule because of the ruckus at the dock and the repacking that was necessary, but that loss could be made up during the night. It was decided to depend on the wind and save the fuel.

With that, Jacques bid Mack good night. They were due to rendezvous at Northern Freight near the mouth of the St. Joe River. He had no clue as to Arch's success or his travel difficulties. Only time and the leading of the Drinkin' Gourd would help them both. So Jacques shut his eyes for some much needed sleep."

Jacques awoke with a start and knew instantly that something was wrong. He could feel the boat rocking and being tossed by stronger waves than he'd seen when he had given the watch to Mack.

"Sorry, boss!" Mack sighed as Jacques got to the wheelhouse. "I'd a tried to wake ya, but this just came up, and I didn't want to leave the wheel. I didn't know what heading to hold it on to compensate for the wind. I could feel us slipping southward."

Jacques quickly referenced his maps and compass. He was reminded that his mentor, Captain Alex, had warned him to be ever vigilant for unusual weather on Lake Michigan. Navigation was tricky when ships were out of sight of land. When on a river, even a big one like the Mississippi, land was always in view. Likewise, the weather was far more predictable there. These Big Lake storms could blow up quickly and fiercely. This night was already testing Jacques' skill and knowledge.

"Go wake Shorty," he told Mack, "and he'll help you get the steam engine revved back up. We'll need the extra power, for this wind is pushing us off course too quickly."

As Mack headed out, Jacques calculated how far they had drifted off course. He was thankful they had taken down most of the canvas and kept the boiler full of steam. Jacques soon heard the boiler being stoked back to life. By the time there was light appearing in the east, he was back on course. Now with additional power, he was confident that lost time could easily be made up. He laughed and thought how the L'Étoile Polaire was of no help to them in the midst of these clouds. Still, he thanked the Great Spirit for their safety.

The master plan was to arrive at the mouth of the St. Joe in the afternoon. That would give them time to get their bearings in the daylight. The ship carried *regular cargo*, some of which was to be delivered at this stop. They also carried *valuable Cargo*, to be delivered with the rest of the goods at Ferrysburg. Jacques figured they'd have time to make their delivery, then tie up to dockage or anchor in the St. Joe River through the night. The biggest unknown was whether or not Arch would make the rendezvous. If he was held up, they might have to leave and come back under the cloak of darkness. They'd not want to draw any undue attention. Another plan could be to feign needing repairs and thus, stay moored until Arch showed up. There were many possibilities.

Timing was everything. Timing the daylight arrival and deliveries; timing the crucial rendezvous. As the sun peeked from under the moving clouds, Jacques' head was spinning. For the moment, though, all he could concentrate on was anxiously pushing his ship on the corrected heading for the mouth of the St. Joe River.

The wind was coming nearly straight from the west and literally pushed the ship into the harbor at St. Joe. It seemed like a fair sized settlement, lined with a few storefronts along a bustling wharf. Jacques noticed smoke rising from several homes nestled in the woodland along the river and surrounding the settlement.

As Jacques entered the harbor, which was not really a harbor but just the wider mouth of the river, he checked his directions again. They passed a larger schooner along one of the dockages being loaded with fresh cut lumber. Farther along, several small steamers similar to the *L'Étoile Polaire* were docked.

All too soon, with a bit of alarm, Jacques and *L'Étoile Polaire* appeared to be leaving the settlement. However, up ahead on the opposite side of the river, they noticed a dock. Not surprisingly, there was a sign, 'Northern Freight,' on the shabby little warehouse. They maneuvered to that dock and secured their lines. Jacques looked about but saw no one. He busied the men in some food preparation and the inspection of the Cargo. Water and food were always welcome after a long day.

In the waning light of the afternoon sun, Jacques checked his maps and charts. The river was a rather deep passage. Numerous times these estuary harbors at the end of rivers were silted in at their entrance. The

Lake Michigan strong winds pushed back the sand to make marvelous dunes, but these sometimes blocked ship's passages. The *L'Étoile Polaire* had an advantage in that it did not draft much water. Jacques hoped all the entrances were as easy as this one.

Their next stop would be the Grand River harbor at Ferrysburg. Jacques' charts warned of dangers with shifting deposits especially on the south side of the harbor. It was recommended that ships go slightly past the entrance, then turn and enter along the northern shore. Jacques made that note in his head, completing his paperwork while awaiting the arrival of Arch.

He was entering his report in his daily journal, when Jacques heard the sound of a team approaching. He couldn't see them because the foliage near the shore was extremely thick. The team slowed and the horses flared their nostrils as if they had been hurrying. Then silence. He rose to the window of the wheelhouse when another loud noise sounded. Thump, Thump! Jacques jumped to the railing. There he broke into a bold smile as he watched a familiar figure jump aboard.

"Good to see you, Captain. Hope you had a pleasant trip and we didn't make you wait long." Arch returned the welcome smile.

Jacques speedily descended the ladder and the two men shook hands, even closer, exchanging a kind of man-to-man hug with the obligatory pats on the back.

"Arch, it is good to see your ugly face. I must say, tonight it looks rather handsome."

They hit each other mockingly and laughed. They were partners for sure, and they did better together than apart.

"And you too, my friend. Was your inland journey successful?"

"Well," Arch stuttered, and his eyes fell to stare at the ground. "I'm afraid it was not quite as planned."

"What do you mean?" Jacques said anxiously. "Did you and Mr. Schmidt find your Cargo okay?"

"Well, ah, yes, sort of," Arch seemed to be holding something back which was driving Jacques crazy.

"Speak up, man. You've got me on pins and needles!"

"Okay, Mr. Schmidt and I went to the planned rendezvous site. No one was there, so we waited. The next day, a lone rider with a Southern accent rode into camp. We were on the river, so we'd set-up the usual guise with our fishing gear already in the water."

Arch continued, "The man seemed more interested in our fishing success, for he did look a bit gaunt. Maybe he was just hungry. I think he *was* hungry, but for something else, if you get my drift. However, after a few minutes he left. To be sure, though, I followed him. He was slow, and I could move quickly in the brush. He went about a mile and met two other men. I heard him report, 'No one there, only an old Quaker man and his Injun slave. Let's get out of here and report back to the boss.' Then they rode off at a gallop, and I didn't try to follow any farther.

"Schmidt and I stayed at the site on into the next day. About dark of the second day, I heard an owl sound. I answered back but got no reply. I guess it was a real owl. But, maybe only an hour later, I heard the owl again. I answered, and this time I got a reply. Our Cargo had arrived but with an added surprise."

"Well, yes. Go on, man!"

"See, the small group had been escorted to the river by a host from the Ohio River area. Well, ah… she insisted on coming along!"

"She! She who?"

Then without warning came a voice from shore.

"Hello, Captain Bateau. Am I welcome to come aboard?"

"Darlene!" Jacques nearly fell over the rail. "Oh, of course, yes, err... I mean Miss Coffin. Do come aboard. You were escorting this Cargo?"

Mack helped Miss Coffin on board as Jacques and Arch joined her on the deck.

"Yes, Mr. Schmidt and I've worked together before. Because of the specific dangers of that particular group of bounty hunters, we chose to split up. Hopefully, it confused them. It seems to have gotten us all to this point safely. By the way, are Mr. and Mrs. Jackson here now?"

"Yes, Ma'am, I believe that's the name of the family Mr. Schmidt delivered to the dock in Chicago. They came in the shipping container and now are in the hidden bulkhead storage."

"That'll be great, for these folk we escorted are related to them."

Jacques was anxious and hurried the process along.

"Let's get everyone settled, so we can get out of here under cover of darkness. It is not far to their delivery point at Ferrysburg, and we want to arrive near mid-day."

"Yes, they've family there who are freed blacks. They settled there with the gracious invite of one Reverend Ferry. He is a longtime abolitionist pastor who has been settled and working in that area for many years now. He was a loyal friend of my father. I hope I'll be able to bid him greeting when we are there."

Jacques simply replied, "We'll have to see what happens." In his mind he wasn't pleased with this new complication. Yes, he was pleased to see Darlene again. But .... Oh, what a mix-up of feelings flooded his mind. His thoughts were interrupted by a question.

"Speaking of getting settled, where might I rest for the night?" Darlene asked.

Jacques looked at Arch who shrugged his shoulders. Then he caught Mack's eye, who stroked his beard as if he'd come up with some sage idea but said nothing. No help from either of them.

"Well, err…, I guess you can rest here in the wheelhouse while we stop for the night. I can sleep anywhere," Jacques offered.

"Oh, you can?" she replied. "I'm delighted you'll let me use your meager quarters. I've slept in worse places. At least I'll be out of the rain, if there is any."

They smiled at each other and everyone moved on to work. The Cargo families were joyously reunited. Food was shared. In the darkness, Jacques and Arch moved the boat silently out of the harbor using one of the sails.

"This works quite well," Arch observed.

"Glad you approve," Jacques replied.

They moved out into Lake Michigan and set course north. Good winds moved them quickly, and they arrived at the sandbars north of the Grand River channel before midnight. The map was helpful and showed the Grand River had carried a lot of sediment. The predominant southwest winds had washed that sediment into sandbars blocking direct access to the mouth of the river. They anchored and would move into the harbor in the morning from the northwest, coming in around the sandbars.

Now, it was time to rest.

Jacques leaned up against one of the masts. Wrapped in a blanket, he wrote his brief journal entry. Exhausted, he nodded off to sleep.

13

THEY WOKE AT dawn. They got everything and everyone settled, the Cargo hidden, and prepared to move into the harbor. The harbor was long and narrow with the settlement inland about a half a mile. They were curious about the reason the location was so far inland, but that thought left their minds as they approached the unknown wharf area.

There were several schooners tied up at the various wharfs. Many were loaded with lumber, the main product of this area. Some had barrels which Arch explained were probably filled with produce or fruit, mainly apples. There was a high demand for such crops in the Chicago markets. Coming from Chicago, Jacques hoped to pick up a load to take on his return trip. He took note of the location of possible suppliers as they moved farther inland. Then they spotted the now familiar *Northern Freight* sign on an old shabby building.

Arch and Jacques saw it simultaneously. They quickly cut their speed and threw the wheel hard in a full left turn. Darlene gasped and quickly grabbed the rail to keep from being thrown off her feet.

"What are you doing?" she exclaimed as she rushed into the wheelhouse.

Jacques was too busy getting signals from Arch. He didn't answer except to say, "Did you see the signal? No lights in the daylight, but the flags do the trick anyway."

"Ah, no," she mumbled and went out, hurried to the rear, and saw just one flag flying over *Northern Freight*. *Ah, ha*, she noted to herself. She looked up to the Captain who caught her eye. She gave him a deep, broad smile of recognition.

All went well as they made the turn around and headed back toward Lake Michigan. They did not see the activity on the shore that had prompted the change of plans.

"I know of no fugitives arriving here; that is absurd!" Rev. Ferry told the men in his most indignant tone of voice. The men were rough, on horseback, carried guns, and were obviously tired of traveling through this unsettled country.

"We have good information on that fact, Reverend, ah-h, Sir," the leader said. "I respect you, sir, bein' a man of the cloth and all that. You would not try to fool us now. However, it does seem kinda odd there are so many nig…, I mean coloreds working around here. I kinda suspect more's going on here than meets the eye."

"Oh, good sir," Rev. Ferry put on his cheeriest, most patronizing smile. "Good sir, you are free to check any of these men. They are all freed with good papers. Don't be surprised if they're a bit shy. They fear you Southern bounty boys might try to kidnap them, papers or not."

"Well, Reverend, Sir, our intentions are totally legit. We simply be searchin' for a family who is fugitives from our boss's plantation in Kentucky. I have all the information right here in my papers. I believe their names is Robinson, 'cuz my boss's name's Robinson and he named them, you know."

"Ah, yes, I'm sure you are quite legitimate, but we have had a variety of questionable experiences, so excuse our caution." With that the bounty hunters followed the Reverend as he looked around the room. The visitors immediately noticed there were six men lining the room, all armed with rifles. He and his men knew how to count and their being outnumbered was noted.

"Well, thank you, Reverend, for your hospitality. I think we'll go get some food ta' eat somewhere. We's plenty tired from the trail. I think we'll rest some and head back south."

"Make yourselves at home, gentlemen. The Hanson House across the way has good food and reasonable rates. One of my men would gladly show you the way if you wish."

Looking again at the six rifles, the leader responded, "Ah, no sir, I believe we can find our own way across the street alone."

"Well then, good day, gentlemen."

Rev. Ferry whispered to two of his men. They left quickly from a side door and positioned themselves at the Hanson House to keep watch. Then he called over his foreman, "Phillip, go out and take down the flag. They won't be safe here with the bounty hunters in town."

As Jacques and the crew approached Lake Michigan at the mouth of the river, Arch spoke up. "What is the new plan, Captain?"

Jacques didn't respond. He noticed a small skiff with two oarsmen coming near to them from the north shore. "I think we may have our answer soon." He pointed to the skiff. "Go down on deck. I'm sure our new directions will be here shortly."

Arch quickly descended the ladder and stood at the rail near the bow. The skiff came about ten feet from the ship. Then one of the men swung a rope over his head. He let go and the rope's weighted end twirled around two or three times, and something clunked onto the deck. The skiff quickly turned and hurried to the shore out of view, no words, no wave, just business.

Arch retrieved the missile. It was simply a rock wrapped with an oiled paper tied to the end of the rope. He quickly returned to the wheelhouse. Darlene had joined Jacques and Arch there as she had been roused by the loud thunk on the deck. Her over-anxious spirit bubbled over.

"Well, hurry and open it. We need some new directions!"

"Be patient, Miss," Jacques chided her with a smile. He seemed to be purposefully taking his own sweet time. One might guess he was being slow just to tease her.

Jacques opened the paper and read it. Then he passed it around so all three were in on the new plan. Jacques moved over to the map and motioned for everyone to look. "Here we are," as he pointed out the Grand River Harbor. "North about ten or twelve miles is the Black Lake inlet where only small boats can enter. Luckily, with our draft, we will be able to do just that. It'll be close, but doable."

The note went on to briefly explain that the awaiting family in Ferrysburg would go north by land to the Dickson Trading Post. They would not leave right away. The party planned to arrive at the trading post late the next day, so as to not arouse suspicion.

Arch spoke up. "Yes, Mel Dickson and his Indian wife are friends of my family. He has been trading in the area of Black Lake for many years. He is a true friend and active in our work. They will be good hosts, even if the Ferrysburg relatives have to wait there a couple of days so as not to draw undo attention.

Jacques pointed out on the map where it showed a small mill on the left just inside the Black Lake inlet. "We'll pull into that wharf about dusk. There are supportive friends close by."

Darlene shook her head in amazement. "It is so reassuring to know there are friends and supporters around every corner. Are you sure our Cargo will be safe there?"

Jacques smiled. "The farm across from the mill is owned by the son of none other than our Captain Walker."

They all nodded in recognition. If Levi Coffin was famous as the President of the Underground Railroad, then Captain Walker would be the second most famous, having added the water transportation to the movement of fugitives.

"Here my father and Captain Walker are back working together even if they don't know it. They would both be pleased at how their work comes full circle," Darlene commented and smiled.

Jacques navigated the ship to the inlet. All went well, though *L'Étoile Polaire* barely made it through the shallow entrance to Black Lake. It would have been better if they could have dropped some of the regular cargo in Ferrysburg as originally planned, but so far, so good.

It was dark when the shadowy figures were moved from the boat toward the lumber piles beside the mill. Everyone was impressed with the carefully hidden entrance and the spacious hiding place there. From the outside, it appeared to be just a pile of stacked lumber like all the others, but clever people have clever ideas. After all of the Jackson family were safely hidden and fed, everyone breathed a sigh of relief. They had accomplished their mission.

"BANG. BANG!" Jacques was roused from where he was sleeping on the deck near the mast. He reached under his knapsack and retrieved his revolver. He looked out and saw two men standing on the dock.

One was holstering his pistol. By now several of the crew were beside Jacques who moved to the rail.

"You the captain of this here ship?" one man demanded.

"Why, yes sir," Jacques answered in his best Southern drawl. "What do ya' all need?"

"What are you carrying? Got papers?"

"Excuse me for asking, Sir, but who might you be? I am Captain Jacques Bateau, and yes, this is my ship."

"I'm the sheriff around here, and we received a warning that you might be carrying fugitives. Some men in Ferrysburg spotted your boat and asked me to check. That's why we're here. Now do you have papers or not?"

"Why, yes, sir. I'll retrieve them from the wheelhouse. I'll be right back." Jacques handed his pistol to Arch and hurried up the ladder. Darlene, who had overheard the conversation, met him at the top with the papers he needed.

"Here, sir," Jacques said as he quickly returned. The ship was a bit higher than the dock, so Arch shimmied down the bow line and gave the envelope to the sheriff who looked it over quickly.

"Says here you are delivering to Muskegon. Why are you here?"

Jacques again poured on his southern charm.

"I'm embarrassed to say that I've never sailed in these waters, and I guess I landed one inlet too soon."

"Bah," the sheriff grunted. He read some more of the papers and handed them back to Arch. "Thanks, Injun," he said, not noticing the wince in Arch's eye upon hearing the derogatory words.

"Well, Captain, you wouldn't mind if my man here, Jones, came aboard for a look see, would ya?"

"Of course not, Sir," Jacques replied.

Arch helped Mr. Jones aboard. He resisted his urge to 'accidentally' dunk Mr. Jones in the lake. Mr. Jones snooped around. He even went down in the forward hold. When he returned, Jacques was there on deck to greet him.

"Find it all to your liking, Mr. Jones?"

"Ya. But this is one funny riggin' – two small masts and also, a steam engine. Don't make much sense ta me. Don't ya find that odd, Sheriff?" He hollered his questions back to his partner on the dock.

Jacques shared with both men that he was fore-warned about the dangerous and quick storms he might encounter on Lake Michigan. One of his captain friends had recommended the double power idea so he wouldn't get caught out on the Lake. Mr. Jones and the sheriff nodded like they understood what he was talking about.

"Seems clear to me, Ed," Mr. Jones yelled down. He then departed and barely missed falling in all by himself with no help from Arch.

"Okay, Captain," the sheriff called. "I hope you can get out the shallow inlet and on to Muskegon."

"Thank you, sir." Jacques smiled and waved as the sheriff and his helper drove off to the northeast. Everyone exchanged glances and smiles.

"Where'd that Southern drawl come from?" Darlene smiled, giving her own version of a Southern belle.

"Oh, I bet you've used that Southern belle act once or twice yourself, haven't you?"

"Oh, whatever do you mean, sir?" Darlene smiled and batted her eyes. That made everyone laugh. A bit of comic relief was a wonderful gift in the midst of their tension filled mission.

Late that night a skiff silently docked at the backside of the mill. Cargo was removed from their hiding place and transported across to the

Walker farm. Before the second trip ferried the last of the Cargo, the oldest man in the group stepped forward.

"Captain Jacques, Miss Coffin, and all the rest of youse, I's and my family is deeply 'debted to you'all. We's walked a mighty long way, but you gave us passage and saved our feet from grief. You have brought us blessing upon blessing. We's goin'a meet my older brother soon at that tradin' post. He's a freed man and he'll be a helpin' us get to Ontario. You'alls have risked life and limb fo' us. I's don't know how I can thank you's enough. What I's will do is pray. I be a mighty good pray-er and I's know's God's a lookin' out for all of us. I's praying God'll spread a mighty blessin' over you'all as we be partin'."

Jacques and the old man shook hands and hugged one another. The man moved quickly to the skiff, and it disappeared into the darkness. Jacques and the crew stood in silence on the deck. Finally, Arch spoke up.

"I guess the Great Spirit has been watching over all of us. We'll ask it to continue to guide this Jackson family to safety."

They agreed with the sentiment with nods and grunts from all.

Jacques' mind raced back to the old days. He thought of the paddle with the Indian drawings. He remembered the times the Great Spirit felt close and had blessed him growing up. He remembered especially his father, Marc. He looked up in the sky, and there was the Big Dipper, L' Étoile Polaire. He smiled, habitually crossed himself, and went with the others, each to his appointed task.

14

WHEN *L'ÉTOILE POLAIRE* returned to the St. Joe River, a familiar man with a broad-brimmed hat and a wide smile greeted them. It was good to see their Quaker friend, Peter, again.

"I'm off now," Darlene said quietly to Jacques. He reached out and took her hand.

"It has been grand having you with us this past week. When might we meet again? Soon I hope?"

"As you know so well, Captain Jacques Bateau, our work keeps us both busy and therefore, we have no idea. But we can exchange letters. You will write, won't you?"

"Yes, but I'm not real good at it."

"Oh, you'll get better after you work that kink out of your neck from sleeping against the mast all week. Thank you, by the way, for letting me use your quarters and your straw tick pillow."

They both smiled and laughed, probably from their own nervousness. Jacques was surprised when Darlene reached up and quickly kissed his cheek. He blushed.

"I must go," she uttered as she hurriedly stepped onto the dock. She climbed into the buggy with Mr. Schmidt, and they disappeared into the darkness of the trees. None of them could tarry, for it might gather unwanted attention. Jacques moved the boat away from the dock and onward for the westerly trip across the southern end of Lake Michigan. Jacques was pleased he had brokered a return load of produce for the hungry Chicago populace. Now he had to hurry to prevent spoilage. They powered up the steam engine and also raised the sails. The wind caught the canvas, and they moved out sharply for their journey to Chicago.

They arrived safely at the designated wharf along the Chicago River and delivered their goods. It was a profitable trip, so they were able to re-stock and prepare to go again. In the meantime, they were standing by idly, waiting for new directions and for something to do. They busied themselves with repairs on the ship, but all were getting antsy for more of a mission. After only a few days their answer came in the form of a letter from Rev. Ferry. He had booked them to bring a load of sup-plies back to Ferrysburg. Jacques was surprised, for there was no special Cargo involved this time. However, after the stressful journey they had just experienced, he looked forward to the break.

Jacques followed his directions and loaded the goods from dock #6. Crew members were impressed to be loading from a dock so close to the business of the Chicago Harbor. There were boats everywhere, includ-ing many schooners, mostly loaded with lumber. They passed numer-ous large steamers that carried primarily passengers to their vacation destinations up and down the western coast of Michigan.

Port of Chicago inspections came off without a hitch.

Jacques put his mind to the job at hand. Because his ship was fairly small and his crew fairly inexperienced with Lake Michigan storms, he chose a safer course. He chose not to do the diagonal course across the middle of the lake. Instead, he did as before and followed the shore, chart-ing a course similar to the one on their previous trip to the St. Joe area.

After loading, they left the harbor and moved out steadily. Their travel was uneventful, with no unwanted squalls or storms. In fact, the winds were quite calm, so they proceeded solely on steam. They used up more fuel than they expected, so they pulled into the St. Joe harbor to purchase some cord wood. Soon they found a merchant, completed their transaction, and began loading. Jacques was cautious as usual. He was always on alert observing, paying attention, and being aware of all going on around them. Jacques became concerned with one man. A tall, slim gentleman seemed to be watching them too closely as he leaned against the front of the merchant's office building.

Questions ran through Jacques mind. *Is he suspicious of something? Does he recall our previous visit? Maybe he's a lookout of some kind? Maybe he noticed our activity the last time at the Northern Freight warehouse? Maybe he'd intercepted Miss Coffin and Mr. Schmidt?* Jacques began to worry, for he had not gotten any communication from either of them. *It's only been a couple of weeks, so quit mind racing,* Jacques said under his breath. Besides, their load was entirely legitimate this time; they had nothing to hide. Jacques moved the ship out toward Lake Michigan hopeful that the man meant them no harm.

Their arrival at the Grand River harbor was uneventful. Jacques found Reverend Ferry's dockage in Ferrysburg and tied up. It was late in the day, and another ship was moored on the other side of the dock. Jacques learned that the ship had unloaded and was reloading to leave in the morning. The dock hands would not be available to unload *L'Étoile Polaire* until then, so the crew relaxed. Two crew members asked permission to go ashore for recreation, some food and fun. Cautiously, Jacques agreed. There certainly could not be many rough bars in such a little settlement.

After writing in his journal, Jacques turned down his lamp and dozed off. It was easy to rest with the gentle rocking of the boat. The sky was clear and the stars shone, especially L'Étoile Polaire high in the northern sky. All seemed incredibly peaceful.

Jacques had not been asleep long when Mack, who was on first watch, roused him. Mack whispered, "Captain, wake up. Someone in a buggy just came to our dock."

"Huh? What time is…."

"Must be about midnight, sir," Mack answered and helped the drowsy Captain to his feet.

"Oh, man, I hope those two sailors didn't get in some kind of trouble in town."

Jacques stepped out onto the dark deck. He turned around and turned up the lantern that hung outside the wheelhouse. Lantern in hand, he walked down to the main deck. In the moonlight, he saw a man get out of the buggy and come toward him. He could see the man was not a rough looking guy. He seemed to be wearing a suit and tie. With a quiet voice the man introduced himself, "I am Reverend William Ferry. I know we've not met, but we know some of the same people."

"Pleased to meet you, sir. I am Jacques Bateau. Miss Coffin had said you were a close friend of her father. She wanted to stop when we came back through from our last delivery, but I had brokered a load of produce for a rush transport to Chicago. I'm sure she would send her regrets for having missed you."

"That's very kind of you, Captain." Reverend Ferry looked around nervously. "Captain, I don't like to talk out in the open like this, even if it's the middle of the night. By the way, I'm sorry if I roused you from your sleep. I'm sure you get far too little of that at any one time. However, would you mind coming with me so we can talk more privately?"

Jacques thought for a moment. Then excusing himself, he returned to the ship and talked to Mack who, even though his watch was done, was glad to stay and be in charge while Jacques went with Reverend Ferry.

They boarded Reverend Ferry's buggy and drove away from the dock and up a road that was parallel to the river. Jacques hoped they'd not go far, for if they did, he'd certainly be lost. They only went a short way and pulled up under a large tree. They could see the moon glisten on the water of the river but nothing was moving there that night. They were certainly alone, and the chill in the air was an omen of the fall weather ahead.

"I have an urgent proposal for you, Captain Bateau."

"No, please call me Jacques."

"Okay, Jacques, having you bring that load of goods was only half my reason to have you here. I have some valuable Cargo that needs to move on north to the Traverse City/Northport area. The weather is going to change quickly, and I'm fearful they've been followed. I was hoping you could take them on and head North tomorrow. I know this is a surprise. But as you know, often times our work cannot be planned."

"Of course we're ready to help," Jacques responded eagerly. My only concern is what goods will I have to take north to disguise our fugitives?"

"My idea is that you keep most of the goods you brought and we'll add some more, maybe cord wood. We'll redo the papers for delivery to Northport to my associate, Reverend Smith."

"That sounds workable. There seem to be numerous men of the cloth in our mission."

"Yes, I believe God has spoken clearly about the importance of our work. I'm a graduate of Oberlin College, and several of my associates from there have come North with me. We were all taught by staunch abolitionists and feel we have divine help on our side."

Jacques smiled, "I certainly agree with that."

As they drove back to the ship, they were interrupted by some loud, terrible singing. Reverend Ferry pulled up and they watched Jacques' two wayward sailors stumbling from town to the ship.

"At least they found their way home," Jacques commented, shaking his head in disgust.

With the new plan agreed upon, Reverend Ferry left in his buggy. Jacques went aboard to prepare for some new Cargo.

Within a couple hours, Reverend Ferry returned with five adults. There were three men and two women. They were hurried aboard in the darkness and moved quickly to the bulkhead hiding space. When the dawn appeared, all was quiet.

Jacques was especially glad to roust out the two partying crew members. They complained mightily, but Jacques helped sober them up by dunking their heads in a bucket of cold water. After protesting, they grabbed a couple biscuits and went to work as directed, aching heads and all.

15

THE NEW DAY brought a new mission. Jacques shared the changes with his key crew members, Arch and Mack. The other five would learn as they went along. They had gotten used to plenty of changes after sailing with Captain Jacques for this long.

First, the load had to be redistributed. Goods had to be moved around. The crew emptied out the aft hold and moved those supplies into Reverend Ferry's warehouse. Reverend Ferry had ordered wood, and soon two trailers arrived, loaded heavy with cord wood to be loaded into the empty space. The unloading and reloading took all day, and everyone was tired. Jacques wanted to leave soon as possible, but he needed his crew to be sharp, so he let them rest until pre-dawn the next morning.

Rest was short and, as the light was just starting to streak the eastern sky, they prepared to leave. The lines were loosed and pike poles pushed them away from the dockage and into the river current. Not wanting to draw any attention, they hoisted the sails instead of starting the steam engine. They moved slowly but silently out toward Lake Michigan for the trip north.

As fall approached, the air was getting colder and, with that, the weather was far less predictable. When away from the harbor, the engine was started to give them steady power. They moved along fairly well, hugging the shore where the waves and swells were smaller. On the third day, as they passed clear of the Hamlin Lake Settlement, the clouds turned dark and threatening.

Arch spoke to Jacques. "It doesn't look good. I'm not sure what plans to make. I'm somewhat relieved that there are several small harbors between here and Northport. We may need one tonight by the looks of that sky."

Jacques nodded in agreement as the boat tossed in the deepening swells. The wind had picked up significantly and was seriously slowing their progress. Jacques motioned Arch over to the map. "Yes, the swells have increased a lot in just the last hour. Let's look at the map together."

Being familiar with this area, Arch was a great help. Many of his native tribesman lived along the coast. The boat had already passed Pentwater which Arch spoke of as home to his family, who lived on a newly established reservation to the east about ten miles. There were also other native settlements along the peninsula up toward Northport. Arch assured Jacques they would be okay.

That assurance was welcome, but the lake got rougher. Arch again consulted the map and pointed out a small harbor. It was still daylight, but it wouldn't be for long. They quickly decided to stop at the place on the map called Arcadia.

With winds from the west-northwest, the storm pushed them into the little harbor. The entrance turned right behind a barrier dune and became a safe, snug, protected spot to ride out the stormy night. The water became instantly still and all the crew breathed a sigh of relief. As they approached the settlement, they were curious to see two lanterns on the dock. Recognizing the universal signal for moving of Cargo, maybe it was no accident they had landed here.

Jacques and Arch knew from Reverend Ferry there was an alternative over-land route. They were always preparing alternate plans in case of difficulties. They were especially concerned because Reverend Ferry mentioned that this group of fugitives might have been followed. Jacques had been directed to pull into the Bec Saus harbor a bit further to the north, in case of an emergency. The storm had kept them short of that goal, let alone, Northport.

There were no other ships at the Arcadia dockage. A couple of skiffs and a Native American fishing canoe were tied up at the shore. The arrival of *L'Étoile Polaire* was obviously noticed by the lookout in the Widow's Watch atop a nearby prominent building. It was the largest of the few buildings in the settlement and sat up on the highest ground. All guessed it to be the hotel for the area.

"You stay here," Arch said to Jacques. "I'll go investigate."

Jacques nodded as Arch left for shore. He, Mack, and the rest of the crew busied themselves with food preparations, especially for the Cargo. They had suffered some sea sickness, but it was too dangerous to let them walk about just yet. Jacques stayed especially vigilant in this unfamiliar setting. Something had made him wary when they arrived, so he had docked with the boat facing out of the harbor. Why, he wasn't sure, but better safe than trapped in case they had to leave swiftly. He paced the deck, restless.

It was dark when Arch appeared at the dock accompanied by a young man. They proceeded up to the wheelhouse. Upon arrival Arch introduced the man to Jacques. "This is our Captain, Jacques Bateau. Captain, this is Edward, the Arcadia Innkeeper."

"Nice to meet you, sir. I'm Edward Wilks. Welcome." He extended a friendly hand. They shook and Jacques eyed Arch for some idea of what was happening. Mr. Wilks spoke up.

"We've heard from Reverend Ferry and his associate, Reverend Bailey. Reverend Bailey lives at the Benzonia Academy about ten miles to the northeast of here. There are some bad men combing the area with the belief Reverend Bailey is involved in the transporting of fugitives. Currently, there's a man at the Inn whom I believe to be one of the bounty hunters. He asks far too many questions to be just passing through. Therefore, your plans need to be modified."

"I wonder if this man is one of the same welcoming committee we encountered in Ferrysburg when we visited Reverend Ferry the first time. That was some time back, but those Southern bounty hunters have been known to be that persistent." Jacques and Arch exchanged a knowing glance.

Getting down to business, the three men discussed several alternatives. It was decided to transport the Cargo by land, using the ship as a diversion on to the Bec-Scie harbor at Frankfort. Mr. Wilks had to return to the Inn lest he be missed and raise suspicions. Arch accompanied him and would keep Jacques posted.

At the Inn, some hints were dropped especially for the sake of the ears of the stranger. The pieces were in place.

Later that night near daylight, dark figures left the Arcadia Inn and were hustled to the ship. Hurrying to depart, the crew threw off the lines and prepared to leave.

Just as they were clearing the dock, a man came screaming down the hill from the Inn. Jacques pushed the ship hard out toward Lake Michigan.

"Get back here, you slave stealin' scoundrels! I know you've got them three men I been tailin' and those others, too! I plan to get my money for those fugitives. Stop now!"

Jacques pulled up the sails. The sails snapped and billowed in the wind as the small schooner neared the harbor entrance. BANG! BANG!

Shots rang out from the closest dune and buckshot clattered across the deck. No one was harmed. It confirmed fears that bounty hunters had discovered them. Jacques and his crew sensed they must have been scouted and followed. The bounty hunters were close on their trail.

The wind stayed strong and the *L'Étoile Polaire* dove into the waves as they headed on a northwest tack. They had supplies that were to be delivered now to Frankfort, only a short way up the lake. Would the bounty hunters follow them there? Whoever they were, they were serious AND armed. Jacques and his crew shuddered at the thought of a confrontation.

I'm sure they are renegade bounty hunters," Jacques explained to the crew as they emerged from below deck. "These men follow no laws and ignore all papers. They get paid by the number of Negros they return, whether they are escaped slaves or not."

It was still mostly dark and they felt safe, at least temporarily. One of the sails snapped in the wind, and a crew member reached to quickly adjust the slack in a line.

"What if they follow us to the next stop?" asked Willy, the youngest crew member.

Jacques could hear the fear in his voice and assured him they had nothing to fear. "You know we have nothing to hide. Our cargo of supplies and cord wood are for the Mercantile in Frankfort. We plan to deliver them later in the morning, and we'll do just that."

"But..." Willy stuttered.

Jacques put up his hand.

"You saw for yourselves the wagon going away from the Inn. Our Cargo is no longer on board, but is, as we speak, being safely transported on the way to the next station. That happens to be the home of our new abolitionist friends, the Baileys who live along the Bec-Scie

River. They, too, are surely under some suspicion, so extreme caution is being taken by everyone. We'll decide later, after we land, whether we can safely reload them and take them on to Northport. They may have to be transported overland, if that is the most secure route.

"Now, we'll all just do our work and prepare for our welcome in Frankfort." Jacques smiled as he spoke, reassuring his crew.

"Ya, from some sheriff and that shotgun totin' bounty hunter, I'd expect," one of the crew spoke up.

Jacques and his first mate, Arch looked, nodded, and smiled in agreement with their concern.

16

THE WEATHER HAD not improved, but the wind had, at least, died down. *L'Étoile Polaire* entered the small harbor of the Bec-Scie River. Arch explained it was not a Native American name, but French. Jacques was surprised and had never heard the words in his mother's lessons. Arch went on to explain it was named for the Saw Billed Ducks that were common in the area.

"Oh, yes!" Jacques shared. He now remembered the word for beak was 'bec.' Thus 'billed like a saw'. Now 'Bec-Scie' made sense.

They looked for a dockage and pulled up under the *Northern Freight* sign. They eased the ship to the dock, set their lines, and observed the comfortable little harbor. Like so many of these river mouth harbors, this one was wide with a narrow entrance between tall dunes. The settlement of Frankfort was bigger than Arcadia, but not much. There were two docks with accompanying warehouses. Most of the few ships there were tied up along wharfs, not at protruding docks. A line of store fronts could be seen on a street that ran parallel to the river.

What was most obvious was a large man on a tall black horse with another man and his mount next to him. The second man was more animated and was pointing at their boat and gesturing.

"That's them!" Everyone heard the man hurling accusations as he neared the boat. Jacques caught the eyes of his crew members and signaled them to remain calm. Jacques walked from the wheelhouse, down the ladder, and stood at the rail closest the two men.

"Can I be of some assistance to you, gentlemen?" Jacques inquired.

"Yes. My name is Edward Marshall, and I'm the sheriff in these parts. What is your name, Captain?"

"I am Captain Jacques Bateau, and this is my first visit to your pleasant village. I have a load of merchandise for the local store. We hail out of Chicago, sir."

"Get on with it, Sheriff! I told you to search that ship, for they's a carryin' contraband cargo in the form of fugitive slaves. I've been chasing this group clean from Kentucky." Sheriff Marshall hushed the insistent speaker with a wave of his hand. He then dismounted. After tying up his horse, he spoke to Jacques.

"I'd like to come aboard if I might, Captain?"

"Of course, Sheriff Marshall. My crew will assist you." With that, Mack and Arch helped him aboard. Jacques extended his hand in welcome. But when the bounty hunter tried to follow the sheriff, Mack stood in his path and simply glared at him. That was enough for the man to back down and stand anxiously on the dock.

Jacques shared his papers with the sheriff, who seemed to be satisfied and asked for the shipping invoices. Arch produced those documents and handed them to Sheriff Marshall, who seemed to be a considerate man, even smiling when presented with the requested material.

"Captain, all seems in order here. May I see the aft hold please?" Impressed by the man's kindly manner, Arch hustled the ladder and helped him descend. He only went part way down and could see the hold was stuffed to the overhead with cord wood.

"Humph," the sheriff muttered, "and let's see the forward storage." He descended and looked at the shipping labels on the crates. He agreed they matched the invoices he'd seen on deck. He returned to where Jacques was standing.

"Sorry for your bother, Sheriff Marshall. It seems your friend," (pointing toward the man on shore), "is confused."

The sheriff nodded and added, "He says you were in Arcadia last night. Could I hear an explanation about why you didn't just come here?"

"Yes, sir," Jacques smiled. "We just got scared of the big swells and waves that came on us right before dark. We chose the closest spot, albeit, we might have been able to get here, but being unfamiliar with these parts, I chose the safer route."

"Ya, I can see that. The man on the dock, Mr. Wilson, says he saw you take three people onto your ship late in the evening. He claims they were the fugitives he's seeking. Do you know what he might have seen?"

Jacques looked the sheriff in the eye, and they stared at each other for a short moment. Then Jacques spoke. "Yes, sir. Two of my crew had gone to the Arcadia Inn, ah, for some entertainment. The ladies had plenty of drinks for them, and my first mate here had to go escort them back to the ship. I'd say it was about midnight, Sir."

The sheriff's grim expression softened, and he extended his hand to Jacques. "Well, Captain, I think everything is in order here. I do hope you might stay and enjoy our hospitality."

"We'd like that, Sheriff Marshall, but this weather is bothering us, and we need to get south soon to put up for the winter. But thank you for your kind invitation."

The sheriff moved close to Jacques and spoke softly. "You be sure to say hello to Reverend Bailey for me."

Jacques was caught a bit off guard. The sheriff winked and moved on to return to the dock. The crew could hear some loud exchange going on between Sheriff Marshall and Mr. Wilson complete with threats and name calling. Sheriff Marshall, who was much bigger, finally grabbed Mr. Wilson by the collar and threw him onto his horse. Wilson rode off in a hurry. The sheriff waved back to Jacques as he turned his big black horse toward town.

"Let's get to work," Arch said, to the crew who seemed more interested in the entertainment on the dock than with their tasks. Arch went over to the freight office to clear the unloading. The merchant's workers arrived and off-loaded the merchandise. The cord wood was stacked just off the dock along the edge of the warehouse. Just before the men were finished unloading, a young man approached the ship and asked for Captain Bateau. One of the men hurried onboard and summoned Jacques.

Jacques met the man cordially and was handed a letter. Looking at it briefly, he motioned for the young man to follow as they moved off the dock to a nearby tree. "You report to Reverend Bailey that all is well here. However, there is a hot-headed bounty hunter named Wilson in town with Sheriff Marshall's ear. Therefore, I recommend an alternative be sought for the Cargo. The weather looks to be cold and windy for the next few days, so I think we'll stay here in port for a while. We'll stock up on supplies and fuel. We'll look to hear from Reverend Bailey again soon."

With that, they parted. The young man walked away and disappeared around some buildings. Jacques returned to the ship.

There was a relaxed mood on the ship that evening. The Cargo had been safely delivered into the next set of hands and the ship was in no danger. They would be provisioned in the morning and ready to sail whenever they were called. Jacques and Arch sat together to decide on their next undertaking. Arch explained the territory and the alternative land route to Northport. The route comprised of an overland wagon trail of ten to twelve miles to get on the Boardman River that flows north to the bay of the Grand Traverse, as the Indians call it. Arch went to the map and showed the wide space between Northport, at the northern most tip of the Traverse Peninsula, clear over eastward to the mainland. That landing point was near another Indian village called L'Arbre Croche, the crossed tree. Arch added that many times the weather, along with ever watchful bounty hunters, made it favorable to travel the inland waterways for safety. His concern right now was that the weather was getting cold and the bays of the Traverse Area would freeze before Lake Michigan. Of course, that might make the Cargo's movement limited or difficult, but others were in charge of that.

"What should we do about getting this ship out of here and back south? I don't want to get frozen in this place all winter." Jacques looked worried.

Arch spoke slowly. "I've been tracking the clouds and I fear there is snow coming soon. I have a suggestion."

"I'm all ears," Jacques relied. "I'm not excited about our trip back to Chicago. What kind of cargo can we contract this late in the season?"

With that, Arch outlined his suggestion for wintering with his people about forty miles south, at the harbor called Pentwater. His family had lived on reservation land that had been given to the Grand River Band of Ottawa when they left the Grand River valley in 1856.

After some thought, Jacques considered the ship's need for repairs. There were cracks in seams, much missing caulk, and one mast needed to be replaced. He believed that a stop would be good for everyone. Arch had an uncle who ran a mill in the Pentwater harbor, and the ship could be dry docked there for the winter. The crew men could easily find work in the mills or nearby lumber camps, and Arch would enjoy spending some time with his family.

Arch and Jacques felt good about their new plan. They hoped the wintery weather wouldn't work against them. Maybe they'd be stuck where they were at the harbor of the Bec-scie River. That was not a completely awful idea, but Pentwater seemed the better plan. So that is what they hoped for as they waited in Frankfort for the storm to pass.

17

THE COLD WIND whistled and sleet pellets mixed with the light rain that was falling. It was a rough night for visitors to be out, but the crew was aroused by a call and someone thumping on the side of the ship.

"No, not the sheriff, I hope," Jacques muttered as he rolled out from under his warm blankets.

In this cold weather, Jacques had taken up residence near the boiler. He and the crew found it a very warm and friendly place to congregate. Arch, who had been on watch, knocked on the boiler room door. Hurrying in out of the cold, he ushered in the same young man who'd visited them earlier that day.

"Hello again," Jacques said, trying not to sound too annoyed. "Come, we'll share some hot tea. You look frozen."

"Thank you, sir. I apologize for not introducing myself before. I am Arthur Williams, and I work with Reverend Bailey."

"Good to meet you, Arthur." The gentlemen both shook hands. They sat, drank their tea, and warmed themselves by the boiler.

Arthur spoke first. "Reverend Bailey asked for you and your mate to return to the Academy with me. He'd like to show you his operation and greet you personally. I have a good team and a closed buggy. We'd be there in about an hour."

Jacques and Arch wasted no time. They gathered their things and put on all the heavy clothes they had, for they were not used to the cold weather. They left directions with Mack and moved out into the chilly night.

Arthur was right. His team moved out briskly, and the ride continued without incident.

"Arthur, have you worked for Reverend Bailey long?" Jacques inquired.

He seemed hesitant to answer, or maybe he was just shy. So Jacques supplied some of his own information. "We are originally from the South, but we were assigned to this Lake Michigan route because of our ship. We came here and have been working transporting Cargo up the western coast of Michigan all summer. We were called to come this way and had an incident in Arcadia causing us to seek refuge in your harbor."

Arthur seemed assured by Jacques' explanation of the purpose of their travel. He began by saying he was hoping to be married in the spring to one of Reverend Bailey's students, Elizabeth, also known as Beth. Arthur had lived in the area a bit west of Benzonia. His family owned several boats that worked out of the harbor at Frankfort at the mouth of the River Bec-Scie. He explained the river was named by the Indians for the Saw Billed Ducks that were prevalent in the area. Arch smiled knowingly at Jacques as Arthur told the story. They chatted easily as the drive continued.

As they climbed the last hill, the settlement grew nearer and more houses with dimly lit windows dotted the way. Soon they turned into the drive of a large brick building. The sign at the entrance said, "Benzonia Vocational Academy." They walked up the stairs and were surprised as the door opened before they reached it.

"Hello. I'm Reverend Charles Bailey." The reverend was a slightly round man of mid-age, and he had a fetching smile as he ushered in the visitors. "Welcome to our humble academy here in the woods. I'm sure you gentlemen have many good stories to tell of your work in the South. I would like to share with you tales of our work here in the North. I have an errand to do, so the best way to share will be on the way to the hill. I will explain as we go."

Reverend Bailey turned to Arthur and spoke, "I will take the carriage, son. Thank you for fetching our visitors on such a night. I will need you to prepare several bedding sets and ask the cook to set out food for at least four. We will be having four more fugitive guests later tonight."

Arthur seemed to understand exactly what the reverend meant, but Jacques and Arch exchanged confused looks.

They got into the carriage again, but this time Reverend Bailey snapped the reins over the team. The team had been fed and watered while the men were introducing themselves, so they appeared ready to go. Jacques and Arch both held on tightly to the seat's metal arm rests as they pulled away quickly and turned in the opposite direction from the one in which they had arrived. Reverend Bailey took a road that ran behind several of the settlement buildings. Because of the darkness, Jacques and Arch had not noticed there were several stores and other buildings in the small settlement. The road quickly moved into thick forest making it even darker. Jacques held on and trusted that Reverend Bailey knew his way.

Reverend Bailey picked up the conversation almost immediately. "As you probably already know, we came here from Oberlin College and originally went to Northport to work with Reverend Smith at his station. It was soon apparent we needed another station, for it was too long a stretch from the Arcadia station to Northport. The Bec-Scie was a perfect small-er, secluded river giving access to this area. Thus we set up our "school for people of all means, station, and color." Jacques noted how Reverend Bailey emphasized the *school* as if to imply what they already knew - that it was far more than just a school. He also emphasized the word *color* as if to make the point of their shared work very clear.

The road soon become nothing more than a trail as it twisted and turned. They bumped over roots and nearly tipped on one small stump. But Reverend Bailey knew his way and was a skilled driver. They soon arrived at a small clearing.

"This is it," Reverend Bailey explained as he stopped the rig, got out, and tied the team to a handy tree. "Come, I'll show you our *farm*."

There he goes again, emphasizing farm as if it has more than one mean-ing, Jacques thought.

They walked a short distance to the edge of a hill. There were many trees, but, even in the darkness, one could see the valley dotted with farms here and there. The Reverend explained this was where they grew most of their crops and produce. "Some of the students work here and help us from time to time." The feeling of family closeness was obvious. Then he spoke of his own family.

"In fact my wife, Lorinda, and I have decided this is where we would like to be buried, when that time comes. Don't you think this is a lovely place for a cemetery? Sadly, we have had to bury one of our children and two of my brother's babies here already." He motioned to some small stones on his left, nearer the trees.

Jacques had not had a chance to get in a word, let alone a question, but he spoke up, hesitant to interrupt the Reverend Bailey's story. "But what about your work, sir?" he asked somewhat frustrated.

The Reverend smiled, turned back toward a large barn sitting off near the woods, and took Jacques and Arch there. He then revealed several hidden sections in the barn's lower area and another in the back of the hay-loft with a door completely hidden by hay.

Jacques motioned to the hayloft hiding place. "What about the people we left off in Arcadia? Are they here somewhere?"

"You remember that hot-headed bounty hunter that met you at the dock?" Reverend Bailey asked.

Jacques answered, "With the sheriff, I might add. By the way, he told me to say hello to you when we met. It must be good to have friends like that in this work."

The Reverend smiled, "Yes, Mr. Marshall is a good man. Because of his elected job, he is unable to participate directly, yet he takes great risks. As you know, the Fugitive Slave law of 1850 obliges local law enforcement to aid the bounty hunters in retrieving fugitives. However, supporters here in Michigan have a good record of resisting that law, I am proud to say. I believe his help getting rid of that bounty hunter was just what we needed." The men nodded in agreement.

"In answer to your question, though, no, your Cargo is not here. They are moving on North. We felt it best to get them clear of that snooping bounty hunter, and we sent them overland to be in Northport, hopefully, by this time tomorrow or the next day."

Jacques turned to Arch. "Then we can leave Frankfort anytime, for we won't be needed to continue the voyage north." Turning back to Reverend Bailey, Jacques added, "That is good news, for the weather is worsening, and we'd like to head for our winter quarters near Pentwater as soon as possible."

After their visit with Reverend Bailey, Jacques was in awe of how the Underground Rail network was alive and well in Northern Michigan. The gathering layer of snow, however, was a more immediate concern. The snow blew around as the buggy returned the men to Frankfort. Arch and Jacques were both in a thoughtful mood. *What should we do?*

On the second day at the Frankfort harbor, Arch sent word to his relatives near Pentwater. He was confident everything would be set for the winter, including the ship's storage and repair. Now how could they get out of this harbor which was quickly accumulating ice?

Jacques and Arch kept a watchful eye and studied the clouds overhead. The third day in Frankfort found them still harbor-abound by storms. Walking over to a dune, by Lake Michigan, the lake was churning as black as the clouds. Then their hopes rose when they were surprised by a beautiful sunset. In that sunset, both were reminded of the old saw: *Red sky in the morning, sailors take warning. Red sky at night, sailors delight.*

Their wishes were granted, for in the morning the clouds broke and a filtered sunlight shown. The lake waves diminished, and the men and crew prepared to sail. The crew hurried to finish loading the holds with cord wood. Some cord wood was, of course, for fuel, but the rest could hopefully be sold along the way and thus fund some of the repairs needed on the ship. The day continued to be bright, albeit chilly.

By mid-afternoon, *L'Étoile Polaire* was nearly ready to sail. The crew cook, Smitty Johnson, brought onboard the last of the food, getting some last minute perishables, eggs, bread, and milk, from a local farmer. The wagon arrived from the grocery with an unexpected escort.

"Yo, there, Captain Jacques!" The man hailed Jacques as he got off his tall black horse.

"Sheriff Marshall! What brings you back here? I hope this is a purely social visit, not business." Jacques moved onto the dock, directed some crew members regarding final details, and joined the sheriff. They shook hands and greeted each other smiling.

"I heard Reverend Bailey tried hard to recruit you to his work up here," the sheriff laughed. "He'll get your old southern blood thickened, and then you'll return and join us here in the North Country."

Jacques laughed and shook his head, "No, that won't happen!" Jacques was amazed at how easily he could to talk to the sheriff. He had kind eyes and a charming smile. *I could get to like him as a friend*, Jacques thought.

The sheriff added, "Best you be careful. You know the Reverend has several lady students. Some are his nieces, and I know he's always looking to marry them off. He might have his eye on you."

Jacques laughed, blushed, and looked at the ground. "Yes, we met Beth who is engaged to young Arthur. It was very late during our visit, so we didn't have time to meet any others at the school."

"Yes. You folk do a lot of your work at night, don't you?" Sheriff Marshall remarked slyly. "I am so pleased to have met you. It is such honorable, important work you do. May God bless you in your efforts."

"Thank you, sir, for the compliment," Jacques said. "As you see, we're about ready to shove off. With this convenient break in the weather, we're making a run for Pentwater." About that time, Arch walked up and greeted the sheriff. Jacques spoke, "I'm sorry. You may not have been introduced to my first mate, Arch Maguire. Arch, this is Sheriff Marshall." They both nodded.

"We are going to Pentwater at the invitation of Arch's family who live just east of there."

"Yes, I know some of the native folk who moved up our way, between here and Northport. They are good supporters of our efforts to help the fugitives. I think they feel like fugitives themselves oft times."

Jacques noted Arch's dark eyes studying the sheriff. He was pleased when Arch nodded and smiled. Turning to Jacques, Arch spoke, "Sorry to interrupt you, Captain, but we are steamed up and should go. This break in the weather may not last."

Sheriff Marshall apologized, "I didn't mean to hold you up. Just know you'd be welcome guests at my home anytime."

"That is very kind of you, sir. We'll be back in the spring." They exchanged handshakes. Sheriff Marshall swung easily onto his horse, waved, and trotted off.

"I like him," Arch commented. Both men nodded and jumped aboard.

ON TO FREEDOM

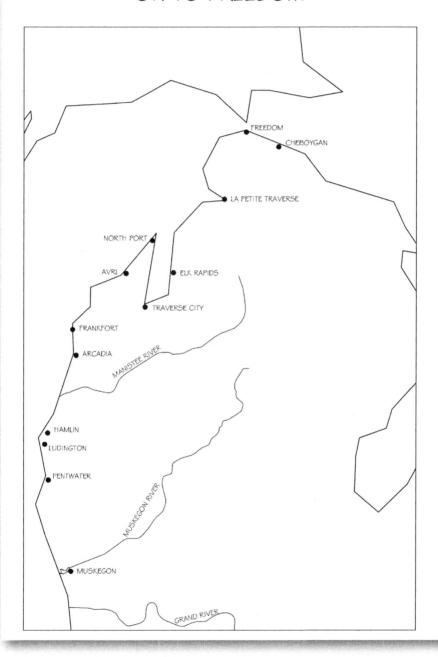

18

L'ETOILE POLAIRE SEEMED glad to leave the icy mooring. The bay was calm, and they headed out of the harbor. Lake Michigan waves were not bad, and the northwest breeze caught the sails as they turned south. The trip went well; they passed Arcadia and those memories made them smile. Their Cargo had been taken overland by Reverend Bailey's people. Jacques breathed a quick prayer of 'safe travel' for they were 'in sight of Freedom,' but winter was coming soon.

Arch pointed to the small harbor entrance, "Remind me to have you talk to one of our elders. He knows many legends about this area. You may be interested to make another visit next spring. This is an amazing place. See the flock of crows? Especially, remember to ask the elder about the crows."

Jacques' curiosity was piqued, and he made a mental note to make sure to stop there in the spring for an extended visit.

As they had hoped, they were able to sell half of the cord wood to another steamer docked at Hamlin Settlement near the Pere Marquette River harbor. They didn't stay long, as Jacques pushed his crew to get to Pentwater. They sailed into the narrow but ample harbor at Pentwater just after daylight. They were pleased with the trip that took just under twenty-four hours, even with the unloading stop at night in Hamlin.

Just inside the dune was the Mears and Wilson Lumber Mill, where Arch's uncle worked. Jacques approached their dock, and Arch jumped off to get instructions. Jacques was directed to a mooring along the wharf, east of the mill. Other detailed arrangements would be made after everyone was settled. Arch was always vigilant. He was disturbed when he observed a man watching them closely from the corner of a warehouse nearby. When he looked again, the man was gone. *Too much worrying*, he told himself.

That evening after most were settled, Jacques and Arch stood at the rail of the wheelhouse. Suddenly Arch tapped Jacques' arm and pointed. They both noticed two men. One man was talking to the other man and gesturing toward the ship. Just as quickly, they disappeared. Both Jacques and Arch were used to being on high alert, and they didn't shrug off the happening as inconsequential. Both agreed they should be extra guarded and probably should be armed, just in case.

Following their arrival in Pentwater, there was a flurry of activity. The worry about the two strange men soon slipped to the back of their minds. Arch's uncle, Ed Mitchell, basically took charge of the boat details. Arch's mother arrived in a wagon driven by a young woman. The younger woman was dressed in what Jacques would describe as native dress that being a buckskin long coat and buckskin high moccasins. He noted she was very beautiful. Arch was strangely distant. He introduced his mother as Ni-maa-maa, who was cordial and a bit shy. None-the-less, she made Jacques know he was welcome to live with them for the winter. There was also a language problem as the family spoke Ojibway or some combination of English and Ojibway.

Jacques was surprised that Arch said nothing to the young woman. So Jacques finally asked him, "Arch, why have you not introduced me to the young lady?"

Arch seemed tongue-tied. "Oh, well, ah, okay." He pulled Jacques over to the wagon. The girl looked away as they neared. Arch spoke to her in Ojibway. She looked up and her dark eyes darted from one man to the other, but finally settled on Arch.

"Ah...this is my Captain, Jacques," Arch said as he motioned to Jacques. Jacques bowed slightly and tipped his cap.

"Ah...and this is my cousin, Star Bright. Her name is actually Ma-wish-ing-qua, but you can call her Star."

Her shyness seemed to disappear. She offered her hand to Jacques, and spoke, "I'm very glad to meet you. I know you are a brave Captain, for you have brought To-Ma-Ho home to me, or I mean to us." The girl spoke English very well. A surprised Jacques blushed and shook her delicate hand.

What did she just say? Echoed in Jacques' head. *Did she say bring Arch back to 'me'? Did Star just call Arch by another name? To-ma-ho?* He thought. *I'll have to ask Arch. I wonder if it's connected with 'Tomahawk' nickname Captain Alex had spoken of years ago.* His wandering thoughts were suddenly interrupted.

"We must go," Arch announced seemingly to everyone. "Our main gear is already in the wagon. We will return for more soon. We will be back and forth often getting the work done."

With that, the group loaded onto the wagon. This time Arch drove, and Star and Jacques sat on boxes that were set just behind the wagon seat. Jacques was again struck by the woman's natural beauty and puzzled by her shyness. She never looked at him nor spoke a word. Jacques began to notice the natural beauty of the surrounding area as they moved eastward away from the Pentwater settlement. The hills were mostly covered by bare trees by now with the leaves blowing about as they moved down the road. They passed some large areas of stumps where the timber had recently been harvested. The land had a gentle roll and a wonderful open, clear freshness that filled his nostrils and set his mind at a peace, a feeling he was not used to. Jacques breathed deeply and felt the fresh air in his lungs. *Maybe this layover is just what I need.* He glanced at the young woman, but his mind was thinking of Darlene. They had exchanged only one letter since they had been together in St. Joe. That was nearly two months ago. His business had taken first priority, and he chastised himself, promising to write a letter that very night.

The trail was well traveled, but rather rough. As they jostled along, Jacques finally asked Arch, "Does your family own all this land?"

Arch talked loudly over his shoulder. "No. The reservation land is up ahead about five miles. The Bureau of Indian Affairs set this reservation up to their advantage. There is no real reservation land held by the tribe; many other tribes have land, but ours doesn't. Here, the Bureau assigned and deeded forty acres to every adult man and woman individually."

"That sounds generous. Why is it to their advantage? I can tell you don't agree with their plan."

"I don't. My concern is simply that with a little liquor and a few bucks, many of the people have already lost their land to unscrupulous buyers. I am afraid that if too many are swindled or sell their land, we will have no place left for our people.

"The Governing Council works to stop that practice. Our chief, Chief Cob-Moo-Sa, and the other leaders try to keep people from having their land stolen, but they can't do much, since the tribe doesn't own the land. People are free to make their own deals and their own mistakes. It has not worked out to our advantage.

"Oh, I see." Jacques mused as he tried to understand the complicated issue Arch's people faced.

All this heavy thinking was put aside as they pulled into a settlement with a variety of houses and a church. People came out to greet the guests. Most seemed glad to see Arch's return and chattered excitedly. They patted backs and hugged heartily. Jacques stayed out of the fracas and unloaded the bags and boxes.

He stood there bewildered when Star touched his arm and, picking up some of the luggage, motioned for him to follow her. She went past the first small house to a small building in the rear. She put down a bag and opened the door. It was dark in the cabin, and Jacques stood outside confused.

Then Star lit a match and a lamp's light brightened the room. Entering, Jacques noticed the lamp sat on a table in the middle of the room. Star retrieved the bags she carried and set them on the table. She turned to Jacques and spoke. "This cabin is for you and ah…To-Ma-Ho," and she pointed to two bunks. The bunks were built along the back two walls. "One for each," she said.

"This is very kind," Jacques said, but before he could say any more, she was gone.

He surveyed the cabin area. On one wall near one bunk was a counter and small sink with a cupboard hanging above. He assumed that to be their simple kitchen. In the other corner behind the door was a wood stove, and he felt thankful for the heat. He, too, set his boxes on the table nearly tipping over the lamp. So he wisely moved the boxes over beside one of the bunks. He went to the stove and opened the door to some red coals.

This will be enough, he thought. He noticed wood stacked along the wall and put two pieces on the coals. *There will be more heat in a minute*, and he rubbed his cold hands together briskly.

Suddenly, Arch barged in. "There you are! I am sorry I lost you in all the family homecoming hubbub. Come now, so I can introduce you."

Jacques followed Arch. He'd never seen him so excited and animated. Arch pulled him into the front, larger cabin. "This is my father, Chief Cob-Moo-Sa. Father, this is my friend, Captain Jacques Bateau."

"What? Your father is the Chief?" Not sure of the proper etiquette, Jacques took off his cap and said, "Pleased to meet you, Chief."

The Chief looked him up and down with his dark eyes and heavy eyebrows. Then, as he rose from his chair, a huge smile lit up his face. He took Jacques' outstretched hand in both of his large hands. "Oh, brave Captain. I am so glad to meet you and have you in my humble home. I want you to feel this is your home now, too." Looking at Arch, the man still holding Jacques' hand said in a choked voice, "And thank you for the safe return of my son, To-Ma-Ho, whom you call Arch."

"Thank you for your kindness, sir," was all Jacques could say. The man turned to Arch, and with no words, they suddenly were in a close embrace. They stayed that way for several long moments. Jacques began to feel there was more to this story than he knew.

With the initial uproar over, Arch and Jacques settled into their new cabin.

Jacques spoke to Arch, "I have a question. They call you To-Ma-Ho, correct? Is that related to the Tomahawk nickname? You said you would tell me about that sometime."

Arch looked at Jacques with his deep eyes, then grinned. "You've discovered my secret. Actually, it was a nickname given me by some white boys at the school I attended. I never thought much about it."

"Sounds like a bit of Indian stereotyping to me," Jacques commented.

"Naw, I doubt it," Arch said, and that was all that was needed to be said. They unpacked and settled in.

Arch's mother, whom everyone seemed to call 'Ni-Maa-Maa', soon had a meal ready, and they sat enjoying the food and the company. Some of the food was new to Jacques. He did not recognized the grilled fish. Not knowing any better, he thought it must be salmon. Arch informed him there were no salmon in Lake Michigan; this was Lake Trout. The stew vegetables were common, but the meat was not familiar. Arch joked and told him it was squirrel and rabbit. Jacques didn't mind. Hunger overcomes most any food prejudices. They feasted well after a long, long day of new beginnings.

Soon Arch and Jacques settled into a regular routine. They found very little need to cook for Arch's mother insisted that was her job. Arch and Jacques found their new cabin adequate, but cramped. The Chief arranged for Arch and Jacques to have horses and a wagon at their disposal.

Every other day, Jacques returned to the ship. Much had to be done to prepare the ship for dry-dock, so the crew stayed to help with the work. However, they were anxious about what was next for them. After the ship had been emptied, the masts were removed to storage. One mast needed repair and was set aside. Arch's uncle made a space near the mill for the ships' dry-dock. Finally, all was ready. Teams were on site along with many logs for rolling. Arch's uncle, Mr. Mitchell, certainly knew what he was doing and engineered the whole process. Jacques was very thankful for his assistance and expertise.

The ship was finally in place. Braces were secured and a scaffolding was built around the outside partially to continue repairs but also to serve as a ladder allowing the crew to get on and off the ship now that it was out of the water. Two of Jacques' original crew, Jonathon and Peter, chose to stay in Pentwater to work on the boat. Being from the south, they did not relish working out-of-doors throughout the winter. They would stay with Mr. Mitchell's mill hands in their bunkhouse. They would work on repairs for *L'Étoile Polaire*, but could also act as her lookouts and security. As satisfying men's stomachs was key to success in the woods, Smitty, the cook, quickly found a job at a nearby lumber camp. Several of the other crew members found work there also.

One of the crew, Willy Jacks, the youngest, decided he would return to his family in the Chicago area. He got on the last steamer leaving the nearby port of Ludington. Jacques hoped he might return next year. Willy had learned a lot and was becoming a good sailor. Many of the crew gave Willy letters to take back to their loved ones or to post when he got back to the city. Among those letters was one addressed to Miss Darlene Babcock Coffin.

19

O<small>NE SUNNY DAY</small>, Arch suggested that he and Jacques go for a walk. Jacques was interested in discovering more about the area, so he readily agreed. They packed a small lunch and headed out into the crisp, bright early winter day. Some snow had fallen. Leaves were still on some trees while others were blowing about with the snow. The breeze was gentle and the sun was bright.

They walked on going nowhere in particular. Soon they found themselves ambling down a rustic two-track road. They could still make out the tracks under the light snow piled about.

"Where are we going?" Jacques spoke to Arch.

"Don't know," was the terse answer from the man of few words who had become Jacques' closest friend.

Jacques' mind gradually relaxed and then wandered. *How long has it been since I walked with no destination? How long has it been since I really relaxed?* Jacques had a very important, dangerous job; he was always wary and on the alert. He was always looking, suspecting, planning, and worrying about what might happen next. But this day, the farther they walked, the farther behind Jacques left those burdens. This day they walked in silence. The air was cold, but the sunshine lifted their grey spirits.

The wind rustled through the oak leaves that clung to the skeleton trees, trees at rest, appearing dead, but only waiting. Eventually Jacques and Arch came to a small pond. They walked along the edge until they reached the outlet creek. Beavers had built a dam across this stream which caused the pond to form. The pond protected their lodge. Jacques stopped and absorbed the serene scene. *I think I've spent more time observing things since we arrived here than I have in a long time. This is amazing.* They walked along the stream for a while and then stopped for a break.

"Fish much?" Arch spoke.

"What did you say?" Jacques was pulled back from his self-induced daydream.

"I asked, do you fish much?"

Jacques laughed sarcastically. Jacques then shared with Arch his story. It had been years since he and his father had fished back in the bayou. Marc had taught young Jacques how to fish for food in order to survive.

Arch explained that it was very nearly the same for him. He and his people depended largely on wild game for food. The fish were just another of the game foods that they ate regularly. He shared that some of his relatives living farther north fished Lake Michigan with nets. That was new to Jacques, and he listened intently. Arch explained how they fished, how they dried the fish on racks, and then how they traded the fish to the settlers for goods they could not make for themselves.

The two men paused, enjoying the silence. Like children, they picked up stones and threw them into the rippling currents.

"How did you get into this work with fugitives?" Jacques inquired of Arch.

"First," Arch began, "the fugitives are a lot like us. The white man doesn't like us, and they don't like Negroes. To our advantage, the white man must be afraid of us for they never come out here. Therefore, the fugitive slaves are safe here. Some even choose to stay. You'll meet some who, like yourself, have chosen to winter here. Some have skills at clearing land and are working in the woods. Lumbermen aren't worried about their color, only about how hard they're willing to work."

Suddenly, a fish jumped and flopped on the water. Both men jumped and tensed, searching about for danger. Looking at each other, they laughed. *I guess we both need to relax. This winter break will be good for both of us,* Jacques thought.

The days passed routinely. The work on the ship progressed slowly, but there was no hurry. However, Jacques was tense about something he couldn't put his finger on. Arch's 'cousin' Star was often at the cabin. Jacques observed some eye contact and shy smiles exchanged between Star and Arch. One day when Jacques walked into their shared cabin, Arch and Star were sitting at the table. Jacques was surprised to see tears running down Arch's cheeks. He quickly excused himself and backed out the door.

That night Jacques had a man-to-man talk with Arch. Arch opened up to Jacques that Star was considered his cousin in their culture because there was a familial connection, no matter how distant. He explained he'd known Star since they were young. He always expected they would one day marry. When she was promised in marriage to a chief's son from another band, Arch became heartbroken and had moved away. While he was gone, he met his wife who, coincidentally, turned out to be Star's sister. After they were married... Arch stopped his story.

"I remember the tragic story you told me," Jacques shared softly. "You don't have to share any more pain."

Arch straightened his back. Jacques could see his moist eyes. "No. I'd like to be open with you. You are my only brother. I have no other to share with. I discovered several years ago that Star never married. The man she was promised to was killed by marauders in Indiana. She and her family returned to our band which had moved from the Grand River to this location. I never thought I'd ever see her again."

Jacques interjected, "And now?"

"Now? I'm not sure." Arch rested his head in his folded arms.

"I believe I have part of a solution," Jacques offered. "This cabin is too small for both of us. I think you and I should build another one for me near here. Then we'd each have more privacy. Privacy for you and Star to make future plans. Privacy for me to spread out my charts and maps to research next year's sailing routes."

Arch looked up with a mixture of sadness and hopefulness. "But we are brothers," he choked, his voice cracking with emotion.

"Yes, and that will remain forever. Privacy doesn't mean hiding or moving far away. Will you help me build? We could ask your father for a space right here in the settlement. What do you think?"

Arch finally looked up with bright eyes. "I'll ask my father tonight after the meal."

It only took about a week for Jacques and Arch to build a small log cabin. Arch's father, the Chief, had logs already cut, stripped, and stacked. He had intended to build another cabin in the settlement. They notched the logs and, stacking them one by one, built a small twelve foot by twelve foot cabin. One of Arch's cousins was a skilled carpenter, so he expertly cut the opening for the door and two small windows. He built a door and hinged it perfectly. The windows were covered in deer hide, scraped clean and thin to let in light. Jacques built a table along the entire wall for his maps and charts. A built-in cot, sink and cabinet covered the other wall. A couple of chairs and a small table finished out the furnishings. A small wood stove was there for heat and to keep coffee hot. Sooner than expected, Jacques was in his new home. He returned from the next trip to the boat with his stockpile of maps, charts, and his journals.

Arch and Star were his first visitors. Jacques was surprised when Star spoke first. "It is proper in our culture to bring a gift to a new house." Moving forward, she handed a package to Jacques.

"Thank you. Thank you both." Jacques smiled and opened the package. In it were red checkerboard curtains and a tablecloth to match. Jacques held them up to admire.

"Yes, I made them," Star blushed and smiled. "They are a small thank you for bringing To-ma-ho back to me." She took Arch's arm and they left together smiling shyly.

Privacy was a good thing. Jacques was able to work on his charts. Arch and Star were able to grow closer. But the privacy had an unintended outcome.

One evening several days later, Jacques was working late into the night on his plans. Hours earlier Arch had yawned and excused himself. Eventually, Jacques yawned, stretched his arms, and went to bed. He fell quickly into a deep sleep.

It was nearly his downfall that he slept so soundly. In the middle of the night, he was awakened by someone wrestling a burlap bag over his head and wrapping his arms tightly with a rope. He struggled out of the fog of sleep. Before he could call out, his world went black from a hard blow to the back of his head.

Jacques woke drowsily sitting on the ground against a tree. He opened his eyes slowly and surveyed the area around him. His hands were tied and his legs were shackled loosely. His hands were strung on a tether rope that also tethered three horses. This was a common system his father Marc had shown him years earlier. It was like an alarm system. If the prisoner moved, the horses would spook, stomp, or whinny, arousing the others. The only light was from a large fire to his left. With that light, he could make out two men sitting near the fire. A third man was sitting not far away on the opposite side of the tree. His rifle was draped on his lap. Jacques did not move.

Suddenly the taller of the two at the fire got up and approached the tree. "Oh, I see our tough man is awake." He kicked Jacques with his boot. "You'll fetch a pretty price back south. You stole my bounty, and you'll pay. You's as black as them. Ha! You'll sell just fine." With that he kicked Jacques hard again. Jacques must have blacked out. When he awoke, he did not move. He studied every detail around him. He figured they had shackled his feet loosely so he could walk; there did not seem to be a fourth horse available. They were probably planning to move out at daylight. He also noticed that his tree-mate guard was nodding off and dozing.

Suddenly, the quiet scene was interrupted. First, there was a sharp thud as a tomahawk slammed into the tree completely severing the tether rope holding Jacques and the horses. Next came a wild, blood curdling scream from the darkness that totally spooked the horses. They jumped and ran. His tree-mate staggered up and tried to catch the horses. Jacques quickly grabbed the tomahawk and cut his ropes. He then grabbed the gun the guard had dropped. As Jacques rose, he pointed the gun at his 'tree-mate'. Before he could speak, he heard Arch's voice.

"Don't you two even think of moving!" Then another tomahawk sounded, slamming into a large log beside the tall man who had kicked Jacques. "I've got one more that could just as easily split your skull open if you decide to move or make a run for it."

The two men were frozen in place. As they looked up and surveyed the area around the fire, they counted ten rifles pointing at them. The fire's light glinted off the shiny barrels though they could not see the men holding them.

Jacques motioned the third man onto the ground next to the other two. Their two rifles were removed. Arch came out of the darkness, pried his tomahawk loose from the log, and cut the hobbles off Jacques' legs. They both smiled.

"Man, I'm glad to see you," Jacques said to Arch.

Arch replied, "You were easy to find. These three are certainly not Indians. They left a trail even a child could've followed."

Jacques surveyed the three men. "I know you," he said to one of them. "You were with Sheriff Marshall when we landed in Frankfort some months back."

"Ya," the leader of the group sneered. "We's been chasin' youse since Ferrysburg last summer."

"So you're the three Reverend Ferry told us about."

"Ya, so what? I know's what illegal business you're a doin', and I intend to get my money back when I find where you's hidin' them blackies. They need's ta go back south to Kentucky. That's just where you need to go. You and that Injun mate could both pass for darkies. That's just what I'd do, but…"

"Well, Mr. Big Mouth, I'd be a bit more careful who I was bad-mouthin' and callin' Injun." Jacques motioned toward the men holding the rifles to step forward, revealing themselves as Indians. "These men you just insulted don't take kindly to bounty hunters."

"Since your horses have run off, I figure you men better get started walkin' back toward Pentwater, or you're going to freeze out here," Arch said as he kicked out the fire.

"What you makin' to do? Let us go?" Hesitantly, the men slowly rose.

Jacques responded, "I'm not going to lower myself to your level. However, be assured that the law in this area will know of your shenanigans. Also, you'd better be careful of these 'Injuns' you just insulted. This is reservation land. I can't be responsible for what they'd do if they ever caught you in this area again."

Arch and his men faded into the darkness, leading Jacques back toward the settlement. After they'd walked about twenty steps, Arch stopped, smiled at Jacques, and said, "Watch this."

With that, he stepped over to the crest of the hill. The three bounty hunters were still grouped below around the dead fire. Then Arch let out another blood curdling war cry which was echoed by several of his friends. Terrified, the three scattered in the direction of the horses' tracks. Jacques, Arch, and his friends all chuckled.

Jacques patted his friend, Arch, on the back. "I also see that the 'Tomahawk' nickname had some validity behind it."

Arch smiled and replied, "Those horses didn't go far. By the time they catch them and get back here for their saddles, they'll be plenty cold and in no mood for any more mischief tonight. We'll go into Pentwater tomorrow and tell the deputy about these three fools." Arch turned and the whole group headed back toward the settlement.

Jacques looked back to where the men had disappeared. *I don't trust those men one bit,* he thought. *I have a bad feeling about how this is all going to end.*

20

EVERYTHING PRETTY MUCH returned to normal after that incident. The next day, Jacques and Arch dropped into the Sheriff's office in Pentwater. They gave him a long report detailing their encounter with the three men. The deputy shared he had also heard about three strangers in town asking questions.

"Is it your ship that Mr. Mitchell pulled up by the mill?" The deputy asked.

"Yes, sir. I'm Captain Jacques Bateau, and we'll be making repairs over the winter. We're staying here locally 'til the spring shipping season starts. We enjoy your area and would be much obliged if you kept your eye on the ship. Two of my crew members are working for Mr. Mitchell, and they're keeping watch as well. I'm sure we won't be sailing for a few months, so I'd appreciate if you keep watch for anything out of the ordinary."

The deputy nodded in agreement. "You're right about sailing. Although it looks to be a mild winter, even if the big lake doesn't freeze over, those winter waters are mighty rough. I'll be glad to go by the mill and check occasionally. Mr. Mitchell is a good man, and I always enjoy the opportunity to stop and chat. He'll surely help you with all the work you need."

They bid adieu to the deputy, shook hands, and left his office. They went to check the ship and talk to Arch's uncle. They told Mr. Mitchell about the three bounty hunters and asked him and his men to be on alert.

Jacques remarked, "I expect those three have had enough and are long gone. But still, we need to be vigilant."

Arch approached Jacques a few days later with a suggestion. "My brother, you're as tight as a bow-string. Come, it's time we go for a another walk."

Jacques scoffed at his friend's suggestion. *Why, we've walked all over this place these last weeks. Why does he want to take another walk now?* But, he also knew Arch was probably correct, so he agreed.

Arch led the way. There was little or no talk. Both men felt themselves loosening up as they got farther and farther from the settlement and all the hustle and bustle. They stopped to rest on a high spot overlooking a valley where a small creek flowed. Even in its near-frozen state, clear spots of running water showed the creek's path.

Arch spoke up. "This is my favorite spot."

"Why here?" Jacques inquired. "I mean it's beautiful but...."

"This is where my father brought me at a very young age. He left me here, and I was to stay until he returned for me. At first it was, as you say, beautiful. But as darkness came, it became scary. I remember collecting small rocks and huddling behind that tree over there. I suppose I was going to protect myself from some unseen enemy with my rock ammunition. I'm sure I didn't sleep, but I heard the wood's noises all night long. I was scared but somehow secure. The owl sound we use today as a signal reminds me of that night I spent here on this point. I guess the owl sounds remind me of some balance between fear and security."

They sat for a while. Jacques didn't speak or respond to Arch's story. After a while, they got up and walked the ridge and then down into the swamp below. They skirted around the edge so as not to get wet. Soon they came to the stream they'd seen from above.

Moving downstream a short distance, the two men came to a large fallen log and rested there. They had been out for several hours. Arch produced some bread and cheese from his coat and handed a few pieces to Jacques.

"This is the pond we were at back in the fall," Jacques said. "I remember this place as being quiet and calming."

As they ate, Arch asked Jacques a question, "Do you ever relax much?"

It was silent except for some chewing sounds and a poetic gurgling of the small stream. Jacques didn't respond immediately. Finally, he took in a deep breath and sighed. "Arch, I can't remember the last time I just sat on a rock, watched nature, and relaxed. I know what you mean, friend, and I do appreciate you dragging me out here." He took in another deep breath and exhaled. "I feel my stress ebbing away with each deep breath I take. One time, years ago, Captain Alex...Do you remember him?" Arch nodded. "He dropped me off for a full day in Cincinnati. I spent the whole day with Darlene Coffin. Now just to say her name relaxes me." He took another deep breath and exhaled through a broad smile. He reached down retrieving a piece of ice and threw it into the stream.

"I have relaxed since coming here," Arch shared. "Seeing Star, I have been able to unload much pain. Carrying pain is a heavy load."

Arch wrapped the snack and tucked it away in the inside pocket of his coat.

"I think we carry the pains of others, also." Jacques said. "We're forever worried for them. We're always on guard and diligent. Relaxing is not a privilege we get very often. However, I do appreciate you helping me see that I need to take care of myself as much as the Cargo we transport toward Freedom."

Arch nodded in agreement. "Jacques, what are you going to do when this war is over?" Jacques snapped a surprised look at Arch as he continued. "You know this Civil War won't last forever. Talk I hear is all the slaves will be freed when it's over. Therefore, our work will be done. The Underground Rail won't be needed."

Jacques' mind was turning. "I guess I've not thought much about that," he admitted. "When we came north, the war seemed to get farther away. I hear the Union forces are succeeding; it has to end soon."

Arch went on, "A friend of mine from this reservation was recruited along with about twenty-five others to join Company K of the Michigan Sharpshooters. They left this past summer. Now there are several graves at the church to remind us of their sacrifice. It hits close to home."

Jacques was a bit tongue-tied. "How do any of us respond to such loss? I thought of enlisting in the fight, but our work transporting fugitive slaves just swept me right out of the South. The importance of this work captured my passion, and it took precedence. I see it's done the same for you. Otherwise, maybe we'd both be fighting on another battlefield. I choose to think we are winning our own battle of the war, helping some of the victims escape."

Arch was quiet and seemed far away. The friends allowed the silence to hold them without words. Arch spoke first. "One of the graves is Star's brother. She is still in pain over his death. I hope I've been of some comfort to her."

"I'm sure you have been, my friend. I'm sure you have. Be assured she has welcomed you beside her in her suffering. That is surely another reason she's thankful you've returned. What are you going to do? After the war, I mean, but also this spring. I feel you and Star have gotten very close. Do you think you just might stay here?"

Arch gave Jacques a long look. No answer came.

Eventually, Jacques observed that the day was coming to a close as the sun began to set. He got up and prepared to leave. "I will cherish this spot for its peace and quiet. I'll remember, also, this stream that washes away my tension and cares. It makes me realize I need to write some letters. Come on. Let's head back to the settlement."

With that the two men followed the stream for a ways. Then Arch directed them up over the bluff onto an old road, which led them back home. After a welcome meal with Arch's parents, Jacques excused himself to his cabin.

Taking down his writing material, he began to write. *My dearest Darlene, We need to talk about what might happen after our work has ended....* He wrote about his talk with Arch and the imminent end to the war. He did not have any good suggestions for her, but he made it very clear that he wanted his future to include her. That he knew for sure.

The next morning, Jacques was at the stable feeding the horses and cleaning their stalls when he heard a rider approach in a hurry and pull up at the Chief's house. He was hollering something in Ojibway. Soon Jacques heard someone running toward the stable. The door swung open, and Star yelled, "Jacques you must come with me now!"

He put down his work and followed Star, who ran ahead up the hill. They burst into the Chief's front room. "What is it?" Jacques asked anxiously. Looking around, he noticed the grim faces and knew this news would not be good.

Arch stepped forward. Motioning toward the young man sitting at the table with the Chief, he said. "This is my cousin, Lester Mitchell, my uncle's son from the mill. There has been an explosion and a fire."

"Well?" Jacques queried gruffly.

Arch went to Jacques and placed his hand on his shoulder. "Our boat, *L'Étoile Polaire,* is gone."

"No, Oh, no!" Jacques cried. "What happened?"

Arch shared the story as it had been brought to them by Lester. "The deputy sheriff heard an explosion in the direction of the mill about dawn this morning. When he ran to investigate, he saw two men running away from the ship. He shot in the air for them to stop, but they shot back. The deputy is an excellent shot, so when he wounded one of them, the other stopped and surrendered. They are both in the jail now."

"Who...? Does he know them?" Jacques stammered for answers.

Arch hung his head. "They're pretty sure these are the same men who kidnapped you a while back."

Jacques' face began to redden in a boiling rage. He began to shake. Arch tried to calm his friend down.

Jacques simply said, "I'm going."

Arch said, "I was sure you would want to, so I already have two horses saddled and waiting."

With that, the two ran out of the house, quickly mounted, and galloped off toward town. They knew enough not to waste their horses, and Arch insisted they slow down a bit. It was very difficult for Jacques, but he complied. Arriving in town, they rode directly to the site of the ship. It was still smoking, but most of it was gone. The fire must have been started in the rear, for all that remained was the bow, proudly displaying its smudged name, *L'Étoile Polaire*. Jacques dismounted and stood in silence. Arch stepped to his side. Jacques dropped to his knees in the snow and Arch heard him mumble, "That's all that remains of my life and my dreams." As he held his head in his hands, his shoulders shook with sobs.

Finally, Jacques rose to his feet, wiping his face. All he said was, "I'm going to the jail."

The two men led their horses up the short block to the small barn with the barred windows that served as a jail in this small hamlet. The deputy met them as they entered. "I am so sorry for your loss. It appears their partner, the third man, died in the explosion as the charges they were setting went off prematurely. Those two," nodding toward the holding cell behind him, "they were lucky they weren't blown to bits along with him."

Jacques stared past the Deputy and caught the eye of the bigger man now sitting with his arm in a sling. Jacques felt his face redden.

"You lousy...!" Jacques rushed at the cell. The deputy and Arch both grabbed and held him back. "I'll kill the little bas...!" Jacques screamed. "I should have killed you when I had a chance!"

"No, Jacques. That won't help anything!" Arch screamed in his ear.

Soon Jacques and his rage went limp. Arch led Jacques out the door into the cool of the morning. Jacques stood beside his horse and rested his head on his saddle. "What will I do?" he said to no one. He and Arch walked with their horses back to the mill area. They met Arch's uncle, Mr. Mitchell, and Jacques' two crewmen who apologized profusely.

Jacques put up his hand. "I don't blame you at all. There was nothing you could have done."

One of the men shared. "We were at breakfast in the bunkhouse. We heard the boom..."

The other man cut in, "I's expect they were watching until we left to go eat and then they set their scheme in motion."

"No, no, don't worry yourselves. The deputy has the culprits securely in jail. We'll let the law take care of them. The third man was blown up with the ship while setting the explosives. I'll let you know what'll happen next as soon as I get that figured out. Mr. Mitchell, we'll settle up accounts with you. You'll be paid whatever is owed for your services. You can count on that."

That said, Jacques and Arch mounted up for a very slow, thoughtful, silent ride back to the settlement. Arch could feel his best friend's pain, but was helpless to make it easier for him.

21

Jacques kept to himself for the next few days. He took most of his meals alone in his cabin. Often the food Star brought him was not touched when she came to retrieve the dishes. Arch came and sat with him occasionally. Since both were quiet men by nature, they shared the bond of their common loss silently. Arch assured the others that Jacques simply needed time to sort things out.

After about a week, Arch was startled by a knock at his door. Opening the door, he saw Jacques standing there.

"Will you ride into town with me today? I have some business and some mail to post."

"Of course I will," Arch answered. "I'll go out and ready the horses. You gather up your papers and meet me at the stable."

After twenty minutes, there was no sign of Jacques. Arch went to Jacques' cabin and gently tapped on the door. "Ready to go?" he asked. Not hearing an answer, he opened the door slightly. Jacques was sitting at the table with his head in his hands. Arch watched as his shoulders shook; he could tell Jacques was sobbing. Arch stepped in and joined Jacques at the table.

Slowly Jacques got control of himself and blew his nose on his large red handkerchief. "I don't know what to do," he stammered. "With no ship, I'm of no use to our mission, no use to anyone, especially no use to myself."

Arch placed a reassuring hand on Jacques' arm. "There are only clouds today, but you know the sun is shining behind those clouds. I know that same sun will shine truth and guidance on you soon."

Jacques looked up at his first mate. "Thank you, my friend. I know time will tell; I don't have all the answers now. But patience is no friend of mine."

The two men rode off toward Pentwater. They chatted some along the way. Mostly Arch tried to keep Jacques' mind off his fears and worries about the future. It seemed to help, for Jacques seemed stronger and more resolved by the time they got to town. Jacques went directly to the mill office to discuss matters with Arch's Uncle Ed. All three men sat and talked around a pot-bellied stove with a steaming pot of coffee on top. Mr. Mitchell informed them that the deputy had finished his investigation, so the site could now be cleared. Arch offered to gather a crew and a couple of teams to handle that task.

"I have some letters to post. One is to the insurance company. Hopefully, I will know soon about their settlement. I promise to make good my debt to you, Mr. Mitchell, and to the mill. Then I will settle up with the crew and pay for their passage back home if needed."

"What about you, Arch?" his uncle asked.

Arch didn't say a word, and his dark, eyebrow-hooded eyes gave not a clue.

We'll only know when he's ready for us to know, thought Jacques. Aloud he continued, "I want you to know I have written to my mother and her husband, Bert, in Louisiana. When I get everything settled and the spring thaw opens the harbors to steamers, I will go there. I may hook up with Burt's crew down there, if they can use me. Whatever happens, I will be starting over."

With a sigh, Jacques rose to his feet. He shook hands and thanked Mr. Mitchell. Jacques and Arch left and went to post the letters.

"How soon do you think we can contact our crew?" Jacques asked Arch. "Do you know where they are?"

Arch nodded. "Yes, most are working close by. Maybe they're having so much fun in this snow, they won't want to go back south."

Jacques did not appreciate Arch's attempt at humor. "Ya," he sneered, "maybe they've been lucky and found a new life already. I wish I was so lucky. Too many gray clouds in my life."

They stopped at the General Store which also served as a post office. Jacques approached the store keeper with his letters.

"Ya knows da mail is plenty slow dees days. Soon da ice be gone and will be better, ya. Ess takin' up ta two weeks ta return, ya know?" He looked over the top of his wire glasses as his brogue rolled musically off his tongue.

Jacques acknowledged his point. "Just do what you can to hurry it along. Most of these are going to Chicago and there's one to Cincinnati."

The store keeper glanced down at Jacques' letters and, looking back up at Jacques, he spoke. "Are ya Mr. Bateau?"

"Yes," Jacques answered.

"Well, I's din't know no one with dat fancy name. I was going to send it with Mr. Arch here, 'cause it be addressed care o' the Chief. Here," and he handed Jacques a letter.

Jacques recognized the hand writing instantly. He desperately wanted to tear it open and read it immediately, but he also wanted his privacy. He shoved the letter into his inner coat pocket. "Let's go," he barked to Arch. The two men mounted and moved out toward the reservation. There were few words spoken on the return trip. Arch was very curious, but he respected his friend's need for silence.

Spring was breaking and the road was slushy. The late afternoon sun peeked out for part of the trip. Just before reaching the reservation, they were met by a group of men and their wagon.

"Going out to start collecting Maple sap," they shared when Arch inquired about their destination.

After the men had passed, Jacques asked, "What's that all about?"

"You southern sailors surely wouldn't know," Arch laughed. Then he explained the age old practice of collecting sap from certain Maple trees. The sap was boiled and boiled to make syrup or sugar. "It is a real spring treat in this area," Arch said, smacking his lips with anticipation. "Yum, yum."

Jacques went silent again. They arrived at the settlement and stabled their horses. It was near dark, so they went to the chief's cabin for some dinner. Jacques spoke only when spoken to and did not seem hungry. He ate little and excused himself soon after eating to return to his cabin.

He stoked up the fire and put on some water for tea. In no time, he and the cabin were both quite warm. Grabbing an oil lantern from the shelf, he lit it, and trimmed the wick. Then he retrieved the letter from his coat and sat at the table with the lantern. He was excited and a good bit bewildered. *Just coincidence*, he thought. *I just posted a letter to her telling of the fire and my plans to return to the South. Odd she'd write me just now.* He opened the letter slowly, savoring the possibility of spending time with her, if only through her words. He read.

"My Dearest Jacques,"

Wow, that feels good to hear! I can only hope she wants to be with me as much as I want to be with her, he thought.

"I know you are devastated by the fire on your boat. I am thankful you and your crew were not injured in any way. I am glad you are with your dear friend, Arch. Please don't be upset with him. Yes, he wrote me immediately. I know you tend to be very private with your pain. But please, please let me sympathize and share. Do write to me soon. Yours, Darlene."

Jacques paused, smiled, and reread the letter. He stared into the flames of the fire and thought of her glowing face. He missed her so much. *Yes*, he thought, *I've kept my pain to myself. I guess my father taught me that. But my mother also showed me I should care for and be cared for by others. This letter makes me feel exceptionally warm inside.*

There was a gentle knock at the door. "Enter," Jacques said.

He was relieved to see it was Arch, who loosened his coat and warmed his hands at the stove. The two, as usual, just sat in silence for a while.

"Thank you," Jacques finally said.

"I figured it must be her letter," Arch replied.

After more silence, Jacques sighed and said, "I wonder what she'll think of my plans to return to the South. I have a small hope she'll come with me."

"And leave her work with the fugitive slaves?" Arch spoke the very words Jacques was asking himself.

"Yes, why would she? I've surely got nothing to offer her." Jacques rested his head in his hands and rubbed his eyes. "But you know, Arch, times are changing. Do you remember last fall when we talked out at the beaver pond? I asked what your plans were when this war was over. Well, it's obvious the war is winding down. General Grant's about got General Lee cornered. And Lincoln's made it clear those Southern slaves will all be freed as soon as it's over. Then there will be no more fugitives."

Silence filled the room again. Then it was Arch's turn to respond. "Yes, but that's at least a year or more away. There are plenty of fugitives for the time being, too many actually. They are getting more and more desperate. There is no food in the South and many are being forced into fighting against the Union forces. They still badly need our help."

After more silence Jacques spoke. "You're right, of course. But…." His voice lowered and he held his head in his hands. "You're right, but I don't think I can be your captain and cohort any longer."

Arch wanted to encourage his Captain, turned brother, and best friend. Arch cleared his throat and spoke. "Ah…I'm not supposed to share this."

With that, Jacques lifted his head. His eyes sparkled with anticipation. "Yes, do go on."

Arch continued, "Darlene has a new plan. Please wait until you hear from her."

Jacques jumped to his feet. "What did you just say? About Darlene? A plan? What are you talking about? You said to wait for her. Is she coming? Coming here?"

Arch quieted Jacques with a wave of his hand and motioned for him to sit again. Jacques did as directed but he was tense, waiting for his friend to explain his last statement.

Arch spoke in his gentle way. "Haste is a raging storm that makes mistakes. Patience is a gentle breeze that clears the mind and redirects the soul. We will know as soon as we are supposed to know. We will wait together."

22

JACQUES WAS NOT ready to sleep. His mind raced. Before his mind had roared with anger over his lost boat and lost hopes. But now, his mind raced with new possibilities. He tried to sleep. He hadn't slept much after the fire and was exhausted. The night's news filled him with hope and finally, he was able to relax. He must have fallen asleep because he was roused by a sharp rap on his door.

Arch's voice called. "Jacques, wake up and hurry to my father's lodge. A messenger has just arrived by foot from Ludington. Hurry!"

With that, the sound of Arch's footsteps disappeared up the hill. Jacques hurried. He threw some water on his face and quickly combed down his mess of hair. He grabbed his coat and proceeded up the hill, past the stable, to the Chief's lodge. He rapped on the door. He heard, "Come in." When he entered, he was greeted warmly by Chief Cob-moo-sa who motioned him to sit at the table. He noticed a stranger already sitting there eating. Arch's mother graciously handed Jacques a cup of steaming coffee and a plate of food.

"Eat," she said, but a smile was all she shared.

He thanked her but wasn't interested in the food. *What is this about? Who is the stranger?* Unfortunately, the others seemed more intent on eating than on sharing. So, he waited. He particularly appreciated the hot coffee, and nursed it impatiently. Finally, the Chief spoke.

"Captain Jacques, this is our cousin, Billy Kidson."

"Nice to meet you, Mr. Kidson," Jacques replied and offered a hand across the narrow table. Mr. Kidson just nodded in the normal, quiet Native manner. Jacques was ready to jump out of his skin with anticipation, but the others dawdled finishing their meal. Jacques remembered Arch's words of the previous evening. *Patience is a gentle breeze that clears the mind and redirects the soul.* He took a deep breath and sipped his coffee in silence.

Eventually, Arch's mother and Star cleared the leftovers and plates. Star smiled broadly at Arch, and Jacques winked at him acknowledging the wonderful warmth they shared. Finally, Arch spoke. "Jacques, you and I need to take a team and wagon to Ludington. We will leave as soon as we can get loaded. My cousin here informs us that the first steamer of the season has arrived there. Since Ludington has a large harbor, the strong current clears the ice there more quickly. We need to go and do some trading."

Jacques was puzzled. The arrival of the first steamer did hasten his plans. *Why do we have to leave immediately, and what will we be trading?* Jacques hoped to have his business affairs settled in a couple of weeks. Then he would clear out and be on his way south. *What was the big urgency now? Taking a two day wagon trip to Ludington hardly seems necessary,* he thought to himself. *I suppose it beats moping around here, so I guess it's okay to go now.* "So, ah… what do you need me to do?" Jacques spoke up attempting to be helpful.

Arch rose from his chair and announced, "We'll get a team and wagon from the stable and load it from the barn by the creek. Maybe we can be out of here by noon." Arch motioned for Jacques to follow. With that Arch and Jacques excused themselves, shook hands with the Chief, and gave a friendly nod to the Chief's cousin, Mr. Kidson.

Outside, Arch gave more directions. "Return to your cabin and pack a few personals. We could be on the trail for more than just an overnight. Bring your blankets and dress extra warm. In one hour be at the stable where Star's brother, Johnny, will have a team ready. Bring the team and wagon to the Mill Creek barn. I'll meet you there."

Jacques took it all in. Albeit a bit confusing, he did as he'd been told. He carried his things to the stable and met Johnny with the wagon and team.

Johnny gave him instructions. "Handle 'um gentle. They's gots tender mouths. Let 'um do the work. You just got to ride so's they know'd yer there."

Jacques placed his bundle behind the wagon seat. He noticed it had taller sides than most of the wagons he'd seen, but that didn't concern him. As he neared the Mill Creek barn, he noticed a flurry of activity. Then Arch and another man threw open the big doors, motioning Jacques to pull into the barn. The horses became a bit jittery as they clomped on the hollow wood floor. Jacques quieted them and pulled to a stop. He set the brake, wrapped the reins about the brake handle, and jumped down. The other men began industriously loading the wagon with furs. Bundles of what species of furs, Jacques didn't know. The wagon was quickly filled and securely covered with a heavy canvas. Arch pulled Jacques aside.

"Please go over to my cabin and bring back my guns and ammunition. Get your own rifle and hand gun as well." Jacques was a bit surprised and balked. Arch took notice and, motioning to the wagon, said, "We have many valuable furs here. Too often thieves and con-men try to intercept Indians carrying merchandise to the trading post. We will be prepared."

Jacques' heart quickened. He had not been expecting a dangerous trip.

"Oh," Arch added, "my mother will have a basket with food. Pick it up and thank her for me."

Jacques began to laugh. "Talk about reversing roles. Listen to who's giving orders to the Captain."

Arch broke into a smile and replied, "Good to see you smile today, brother." Then he gently pushed Jacques on his way out the door.

Soon they were packed and waved goodbye. They traveled north. From his sailing experience, Jacques was keen on his directions and he made mental notes of their trail. They passed through several small communities that Arch explained were all a part of the northern half of the reservation. It was getting dark and cooling down considerably when they pulled up at the edge of a river named for an early priest popular in this part of Michigan, Father Marquette. Arch explained that usually his family would come here, transfer to canoes, and make their way to Ludington by water. Before Jacques could ask the obvious question about why not this time, Arch motioned for him to dismount the wagon. After giving the team some grain and hay and letting them rest for a while, Arch and Jacques walked over to the bridge that crossed the river.

"Wow! I can see why we wouldn't want to be in a canoe in that river," Jacques remarked looking at the swollen stream and listening to its roar.

Arch explained, "You see, in the winter the lumbermen cut logs and pile them at the river bank. When the snows begin to melt and the streams swell, they release the logs to flow downstream to the waiting mills. Even in the moonlight, you can see the river is rolling and churning with logs. That's why we now travel by wagon, not by canoe."

Walking back to the wagon, Arch spoke again, "We'll stop for the night up the trail a bit. Let's get going before we and the horses get too cold."

With that, they gathered up the horses' gear and feed and mounted the wagon. With a snap of the reins, Arch guided the jittery horses over the bridge that spanned the raging river full of clunking logs. It was good to get into the woods away from the thundering roar. Soon Arch pulled the team and wagon off the trail into a small clearing.

"Unhook the team and take them over to the stream by that big willow tree. Don't worry, they're thirsty. They'll help you find the water."

Jacques returned to a warm fire and a make-shift shelter Arch had erected against the wagon. They ate and dozed off. Chills awoke Jacques when the fire burned down to coals. He threw on some more fuel which quickly caught and blazed with heat. It was near dawn when Arch awoke. Together, they took care of their gear, fed and watered the horses again, and hooked them to the wagon. It will be a long day because they want to arrive at the trading post before dark.

"Have your side arm and rifle close at hand. About an hour or so up the trail, I expect we'll have some company." Arch seemed to have complete knowledge of this trail, for which Jacques was deeply grateful.

Daylight brightened the eastern sky as they left their camp and moved out. The two friends talked very little. A short while later Jacques was roused from his day-dreaming by Arch's elbow poking him in the ribs. Jacques noticed a small settlement ahead. Two men outside a small building were standing in the middle of the trail blocking it. Arch pulled the team to a halt just as a third, large-bellied man came out the building caring a jug.

"Howdy, strangers. Do stop and come in for a drink. If it's furs your carrin', I'd be glad to offer you a fair trade and save ya the day's trip all the way over to the tradin' post." The man hoisted the jug toward

Jacques and Arch, but they never moved. Before Arch spoke, he put his rifle over his lap; Jacques fingered his revolver and held it in plain view.

"No thanks, Mister. No dumb Injuns here to ply with your whiskey and have your men there half empty the wagon as you deal with the liquored owners. You and your conniving ways are well known to my tribe. Chief Cob-moo-sa has warned everyone who comes this way. Now we'll be gone. Get out of our way."

The big bellied man nodded to the men in the road. They jumped aside as Arch pushed the team into a quick trot. Jacques stood and kept watch to the rear to make sure no one followed.

"Phew," Jacques let out a sigh of relief. "They've got one slick scheme there. I'm impressed at how hard your father works to keep his people safe. I'm glad you're so knowledgeable, for this sailor would certainly be lost and afloat in this place."

Arch just smiled and snapped the reins again to hurry the team.

The settlement of Ludington was very active when they arrived. Along the river many mills buzzed with the sounds of saws at work. Logs like those they'd seen earlier in the river were being cut into lumber as quickly as possible. Now that the ice had melted, the lumber schooners were anxious to get the lumber to markets, especially to the bustling, growing city of Chicago.

"Whoa," Arch said as he pulled the team up outside the Lakeside Hotel on Main Street. "Let's stop here and get a good meal. The fur trader we seek is a short distance north of this settlement at Hamlin. We'll go there soon."

Jacques dismounted and stretched the stiffness from his body. He'd hardly moved from the wagon when a voice shocked him to attention.

"Captain Jacques Bateau, it's about time you got here."

Jacques jerked around and immediately recognized the young lady standing on the porch. He ran to her, hugged her, and whirled her around to her squeals of glee.

All his questions tumbled out, "Where...When...Why are you here?"

"I came to see you, silly. I need a Captain, and I hear you are unfortunately available," Darlene laughed. Then seeing Arch approach, she pulled herself away from Jacques' grasp. "And here is my favorite co-conspirator!" Darlene hugged Arch who, in spite of his shyness, grinned from ear to ear.

"Conspirator?" Jacques looked back and forth between Arch and Darlene.

Arch shrugged his shoulders. "I told you she had a plan, remember?" Arch smiled as the three old friends savored their time together. "I'll leave you now to get re-acquainted," he said sarcastically climbing aboard the wagon. "I'll take the furs up to the trading post and be back shortly. I know you have a great deal to discuss. You can catch me up over a meal this evening. I'll see you both back here at eight in the dining room."

He was off, and Darlene ushered Jacques toward the lobby. "Come on. I'm getting cold." She hugged his arm as they walked across the porch and into the well-lit lobby. "Come, let's sit and have a warm drink while we get caught up." Darlene led Jacques to a small table in the café and ordered two coffees.

"Darlene, you are such a beautiful sight for these sore eyes! I can't begin to tell you how much I've missed you."

"That's good, Captain Bateau. I enjoy having you tell me how much you've missed me. However, if it all works out, we won't have to be apart any longer."

"What? You're staying? That's fabulous news! Now, I'm dying of curiosity. What are your plans? Arch told me you had something up your sleeve, but he wouldn't say what. Don't be upset with him for letting me in on that small part of your conspiracy."

When Arch returned a little after eight, the two were still at the table in the café. Darlene had produced some papers that Jacques was studying. Both he and Darlene were very animated with excitement. "How about letting me in on the discussion?" Arch said as he pulled off his heavy coat and pulled up a chair.

As the evening progressed, ideas were exchanged. Food tasted better and better as a new vision of a bright future began to replace the darkness of depression that had hovered over Jacques during the last few weeks.

"So, the gist of it is that Reverend Bailey wrote me about the need for another ship to operate at the north end of the Underground Railroad. He and his men were impressed with what you and Arch have accomplished since coming to Chicago. After Reverend Bailey's regular captain got ill and died back in December, I naturally thought of you, Captain Jacques."

Jacques was all smiles. "I thought all my dreams were dead. I have been a captain without a ship. Now you tell me there is a ship without a captain. It looks like a match made in heaven to me." Jacques stood and raised his glass, "A toast to new beginnings!"

"A toast to our new life together," Darlene added glancing coyly at Jacques.

Arch chimed in, "A toast to both of you and what the future holds for all of us." His mind drifted off to Star. *And a toast to our future also,* he said to himself.

"Clink, Clink" sounded as the glasses met.

"Patience is a gentle breeze that clears the mind and redirects the soul." Jacques smiled at the thought.

23

THE THREE-SOME RETURNED to the settlement without incident. The place was alive with a new energy obvious to all. Star had arranged to have Darlene stay with her. They bonded easily and quickly became close friends. The excitement was timed perfectly as spring was upon them. The harbors would soon be clear of ice, and everyone was anxious for there was much to do. Many fugitives were making their way to the North. With the war's end in sight, the South was decimated. There was no food or work; there was nothing left to do but to leave and go north. Slaves who remained were treated more harshly than ever before. Many were forced by their masters to join the Confederate Army and fight against the Union. There were still many in the South who believed the South might win the war. Those were the worst, threatening and harassing all slaves, fugitives or not. If caught leaving, slaves were hauled back to even harsher conditions. Others were killed to set an example.

Jacques and Darlene posted letters to her father and to Reverend Bailey informing them that Jacques was looking forward to joining in their mission to get fugitives to Freedom. Reverend Bailey was thrilled to receive Jacques' response. He and his friend in Northport, Reverend Smith, were busy preparing Jacques' new boat. Everyone was anxious to get it up and running, but there were problems. First, Jacques had to get to Northport. Over land? Most likely his passage would be on the steamer that delivered Darlene because Lake Michigan was free of ice even if inland harbors were not.

Another problem was the ice that still filled most harbors. A large group of fugitives who couldn't travel over the winter were staying with Reverend Bailey. There was an urgency to move them. How could they be transported to a ship on Lake Michigan when harbors of Frankfort or the Traverse Settlement would be locked in ice for several more weeks?

The most pressing problem was Jacques' need to settle up accounts for his old business. When he arrived back at the settlement, he received bad news from the insurance company. The 'small print' in his policy stated that only half of the damages would be paid because his loss was not caused by a natural disaster. It stated 'loss by criminal element' would only be reimbursed at half compensation. Though disheartened, Jacques was able to settle with the mill crew, Mr. Mitchel, and his own sailors.

There was also good news. When Jacques reconnected with his old crew, he was able to recruit four of them, Mack, Jonathan, Peter, and the cook, Smitty Johnson, for his new ship. The new ship was a smaller and could be operated with six, if necessary. After settling all his debts, Jacques was able to pay their passage to Northport, and still he had enough money left to send some back to Chicago for young Willy Jacks.

Arch, Darlene, and Star made their own contributions. Arch would do some overland work with the fugitives or act as a diversion when necessary. Darlene was going on with Jacques to Northport. Star was planning to stay at the reservation, as she had become indispensable to the Chief, functioning as secretary, bookkeeper, and accountant. She urged Arch to return to her soon, but she promised she would be patient for she knew how important this work was to everyone.

Two days before they were scheduled to leave, Arch came up with a plan of his own. That morning dawned clear and sunny, with a warm breeze from the south unlike the winter gusts from the north. He packed some simple food and suggested the four friends take a walk. They needed some relaxation and some time together. They had walked quite a distance enjoying the quiet and signs of coming spring. Always the sailor, on land Jacques was totally confused as to where they were. He didn't worry, however, for he was certain of his guide's abilities. He tried not to fret about the future. His recent days were consumed with details, lookouts, plans, and vigilance. Even now with Darlene beside him, he felt himself on edge.

As they approached the beaver pond where he and Arch had been before, Jacques recognized the location. As before, it was peaceful and serene. With the spring thaw, the pond level was higher than previously. They skirted around the west side and came to the outlet stream. They stopped, pulled up a rock, so to speak, and rested.

Jacques recalled how the last few months had been like the deep roar of a huge waterfall. But here he listened to the gurgle of the stream as it spilled over the beaver cuts and flowed down the creek. Jacques thought back to the fire. His rage had nearly destroyed him. He knew at that point he'd have killed the man who set the explosives. That sound roared in his head, but slowly the gurgling stream took over, and the roar subsided.

Being there with his friends, he felt a new peace. His life was like Spring itself with everything new. Just when he thought all was lost, he and Darlene came up with a fresh, new idea. A new boat, new fugitives needing help -- everything was just like spring – all things new. The deep roar of the waterfall grew very distant. He thanked Arch for helping to 're-orient his soul.' All of the friends appreciated their many blessings, especially each other. They ate, talked, and laughed. They shared a day that might be their last together, at least for a long while. As they trekked back to the settlement, they felt a bitter-sweetness. But mostly they felt hopeful about the unseen adventures ahead.

24

I T WAS A tearful good-bye at the Chief's settlement. All had grown very close through disaster and friendship; all promised to return again soon. Jacques and Darlene loaded up and headed back to Ludington to catch the steamer. They arrived without problems and booked passage the next day. Being the perfect gentleman, there was no doubt that Darlene would be lodged in a state room. Jacques would do okay in passage class on the floor of the lounge. The lake was quite calm although the air was plenty chilly, and they spent most of their time in the lounge together.

They arrived in Northport with a warm welcome from Reverend Smith. He explained that he and Reverend Bailey were close associates. They had originally planned to work together from the Northport area but soon discovered they needed another station a bit farther south. They settled on the area around Benzonia. It would make a good location for the Academy was located near numerous water to help transport their valuable Cargo,

Reverend Smith was anxious to get started. After he settled Darlene at the home of his married daughter, Mary Wolfe, he took Jacques to the mooring. "There it is," the Reverend said, motioning toward a ship named *'Glory'* at the dockage.

Jacques could tell it was not the *L' Étoile Polaire*, but it looked to be sturdy and sea worthy. Jacques examined it from stem to stern. He told Reverend Smith that his crew would be coming the next day and they'd get it going immediately. After his initial inspection, Jacques spoke to the Reverend. "I'm sorry for the previous captain's misfortune. What happened to his crew?"

"A skeleton crew was all he'd gathered," Reverend Smith responded. "They left on the last steamer out of here, just before the ice closed us in. They had no interest in getting stuck up here through the winter with no captain or future prospects. So it is well you have your crew with you."

Jacques explained the arrangements he had made for his crew members when they stayed in Pentwater. Two of the crew, Jonathan and Peter, had stayed to work on the ship. Others, like Mack, had taken temporary placement with lumbering crews. His cook, Smitty, had made himself famous over the winter with his good old-fashioned Southern cooking. Those north woods loggers loved it. "I barely got him away, but he came willingly once he learned his next assignment would be on a wannigan, bouncing down the rivers with a bunch of logs. He was actually glad to return to our mission."

Jacques' crew arrived and got to work. Supplies were loaded and new bulkhead hiding places were built. They did not want their modifications to look new or conspicuous, so they used old weathered boards from a wrecked ship they found nearby. They strengthened the lower timber in the holds. Jacques was below when he discovered several cartons stamped with the letters 'BFG.' He questioned the letters and the ship's name, 'Glory.' *BFG and Glory*, he thought. *There must be something to that, but I don't have time to figure it out now. There's work to be done.*

Mack was especially pleased to reunite with Jacques. He immediately set to work on the steam engine, tuning it over and over. Finally he hollered to Jacques, "It's ready!"

"We'll take it out tomorrow," Jacques announced to the crew.

The next day all went well as they eased *Glory* out into the bay. The lower bay was still full of ice, so Jacques set a southeast course toward what his maps labeled Old Mission Point. It was the tip of a shorter peninsula that cut the bay into two parts. The charts called it The Grand Traverse from the French, La Grande Traversée meaning long trip or travel. Arch had explained before he left how the Indians went across The Grand Traverse in canoes. Sometimes storms made the trip difficult. They would go toward this smaller point and lay up on the lee side away from the wind. The Indians' next destination would be across this bay to a smaller bay called *La Petite Traversée*, the short trip.

Glory handled well and Jacques' experienced crew worked together smoothly. They returned without incident to Northport with their 'maiden voyage' under their belts.

Jacques had lots to learn, particularly about the new sailing waters. After they returned and secured the ship, he stayed at the ship studying his charts and maps. He lost track of the time. He was roused from his concentration by a rap on the wheelhouse door. He opened it to see a tall trim Indian with a wide smile.

"I am Reverend Smith's son-in-law, Payson Wolfe," he said, offering his hand. "The Reverend has sent me for you as our family is ready for dinner. They were worried you might not be well, but Darlene assured us you were probably just studying your charts." He smiled and both laughed easily.

"Pleased to meet you," Jacques responded. "I apologize if I delayed your family's meal. Let me grab my coat and we'll be off." He quickly straightened his work, blew out the lamp, and joined his host. "Your wife must be Mary. She was with her father when we landed. She helped Darlene get settled."

"You're correct," Payson nodded.

Jacques observed Payson, being Native American, was very similar to Arch - well-educated, talented and resourceful. Jacques was pleased to know he was part of their team. They returned to Reverend Smith's home, where Darlene was being entertained by Payson's wife, Mary.

Darlene came over to Jacques as soon as the two men entered the home. "I've been getting a fast education on the work that goes on in this area. My father, Levi Coffin, has been friends and partners with both Reverend Bailey and Reverend Smith. We'll fit right in here."

Jacques loved how she used the pronoun 'we.' *I look forward to working with Darlene for the rest of my life.* He smiled at the warm thought.

Later that evening, Reverend Smith pulled Jacques and Arch aside and explained there was a pressing need. He didn't want to rush Jacques and his crew, but as Jacques already knew, there was special Cargo who had been waylaid for several months because of the winter. He went on. "We have been working for a while now with a special courier in Virginia named Jonas Miller. Jonas is a black fugitive himself. His connection to our area came through a Union Army officer, Colonel Benning, whom he rescued on the Wilderness Battlefield in Virginia. Since then Jonas has gone back twice to help other family members escape the South. Being from the South, Jonas was surprised by and unprepared for our winter up here. His party was laid over for a prolonged stay with our mutual friend, Reverend Bailey."

Jacques replied, "Yes, we met the Reverend one evening when he showed us his *farm* and the special building he'd prepared for fugitives passing through. It must have been hard for them getting through the winter."

"The fugitives got here just after Christmas, as travel became increasingly difficult. Before they could be moved, a bad blizzard set in. They have been with Reverend Bailey ever since." Reverend Smith sighed deeply as he sat back in his chair. The men all considered their course of action.

Jacques spoke first, "Not to jump ahead, but I'm guessing overland travel is still too difficult because of the snow. Therefore, you need us to sail to the Bec-Scie harbor and bring the fugitives here."

"Precisely son, but there's a hitch. Let me show you. Ice still fills the Bec-Scie harbor." Reverend Smith pulled out his maps and talked about possibilities. Arch was very familiar with the area and possible land routes. Jacques could manage the ship route. With the snow and ice clogging the streams and harbors, it would not be easy. But soon the men had developed a plan and were able to return to the ladies, to enjoy their pleasant company along with some hot cider and donuts.

At the end of the evening, Jacques escorted Darlene back to her quarters and explained the details to her. She responded with enthusiasm and shared in the excitement. The next day was spent loading provisions and fine-tuning the steam engine. They also took on additional cord-wood for trade. It would serve as a diversion in case they were questioned. The next morning dawned bright yet cool.

"Where's Arch?" Darlene asked.

"He'll meet us a bit later," Jacques replied somewhat tersely.

Darlene gave him a stern look. She felt like he'd cut her short, but she was getting used to his quirks of personality. *I suppose I best learn all I can about him if we are going to spend the rest of our lives together*, she thought. They were both ready for their new adventure.

25

"SHE'S READY, SIR." Mack yelled at Jacques from the engine hold.
"Let off the lines," Jacques yelled to the crew. In spite of it being
only their second voyage, they moved *Glory* away from the dock with
ease. *Glory* was not as large as the *Polaire*. It was only a steamer with
no auxiliary sails. However, being smaller, it was swifter on the water,
and they made good time to the rendezvous.

Earlier, Arch and Payson Wolfe had set off by land. It was a hard
trek using an ice boat to get down the bay and snowshoes from there on.
They hoped they could meet Jacques before the spring storms began to
blow.

Arch and Payson arrived at Reverend Bailey's on schedule. The
Cargo was to be transported to the small town of Aurl, a bit north of
the Bec-Scie Harbor. There was no particular harbor at Aurl, but more
of a cove. A dockage had been built out into Lake Michigan which was
clear of ice. It was not much, but Jacques would meet them there and
load.

Reverend Bailey arranged for two teams with sleighs to transport
and hide the Cargo, nestled in compartments under the hay. Even in
the very cramped quarters, they knew they could survive the ride to the
lakeshore. Reverend Bailey explained one of their biggest obstacles now
was that their friend, Sheriff Marshall, had been killed in an ambush at

a lumber camp by a deranged man who was now in jail. Justice, courts, and judges moved slowly, even more so in the winter. The people in town would wait until the judge made his rounds later in the spring before court could be convened.

With the helpful sheriff gone, bounty hunters had been sniffing around all winter. The Reverend warned Arch and Payson to be very careful and was relieved to notice that both were armed. As they loaded the Cargo the next morning near daylight, they were introduced to Jonas. Jonas was the leader of the group who had wintered with Reverend Bailey. Jonas was leery of this new water method of transportation, and Reverend Bailey had to do some strong urging to convince Jonas to try it.

Arch and Payson drove the wagons as they set out in the dark of early morning and moved along well for several hours. Somewhere around the Platte Lakes, just after dawn, they stopped at an artesian well where everyone got water, including the horses. The teams had worked especially hard through some badly drifted trails. The caravan moved on with more confidence in the light of the day. The group also able to enjoy a few peeks of the sun through the gray clouds.

Spring was breaking up the ice quickly. Jacques had sailed his ship slowly and carefully. He stayed close to shore so as not to meet any of the large, early spring steamers or be forced to contend with the destructive waves of Lake Michigan. They found the Aurl dockage and eased in slowly. Jacques was concerned that no signal flags were flying. Then he spotted a man running to the dock who told them about a confrontation that had just happened near the mill office.

Shortly before this, Arch had pulled up his team near the top of a slight downgrade where the road entered the settlement. He had signaled to

Payson and pointed out the main mill building where all were to meet. However, there was only one flag flying. The second pole was bare. That was not good. They proceeded on down the grade and veered to the right toward the mill's stable, a short distance beyond the mill. There they inquired about Edward, a name they had been given as a contact person. Just as Edward emerged, two rough looking men came striding into the stable.

"Here are your horses, gentlemen." Edward smiled cordially as he handed each man his reins.

"Ya, ya? Damn it. I was sure we'd find something here. Ever since that sheriff was killed, people been real shy to speak up or help a soul." He prepared to mount his horse when interrupted.

"Hey, how about these wagons? Where'd they come from?" The second man asked no one in particular. "Hey, you there, Injun. Where'd you'all come from?"

Edward jumped in between the men and the wagon. "These men just brought a couple loads of hay for the horses from that storage barn out yonder."

"Oh Ya? Well, maybe you's also farming fugitives!" With that, the man grabbed a pitch fork that stood against the wall. "I'll just check this here load," he announced and stabbed the fork in several times.

"Give it up, Junior," the older man said. "We've got a long ride in this damnable cold. Let's get going." With that, he mounted his horse and handed the other horse's reins to Junior, who growled, cursed, and threw the pitch fork on the ground at Edward's feet. Edward did not move nor did he notice Arch and Payson both had pistols in their hands, hidden at their sides.

"Let's get out of this God-forsaken hole." Both men yanked their horses harshly, spurred them in the ribs, and galloped off.

Arch, Payson, and Edward looked at each other and sighed with relief.

"Did those horrible bounty hunters leave?" asked an older man as he hurried up to the stable from the mill office.

"All is clear now, I believe," Edward answered. "Let's get to the dock immediately."

They rushed out to the dock to find an anxious Jacques and crew. The Cargo was quickly loaded as *Glory* bobbed up and down at the shaky dock. This was dangerous work to do even in the daylight. Too many curious eyes could be watching. Jonas marshalled his people together. Arch and Payson returned the teams and the wagons to the stable and handed them off to Edward.

"We'll be back. God only knows when. We, or maybe Reverend Bailey, will retrieve the horses; hide those wagons with the false bottoms."

Edward nodded in agreement, and the men ran for the boat dock.

Everything was ready, so the boat pushed off as soon as the Arch and Payson leapt onto the deck. As they moved north toward Northport, the waves grew rougher. Not far up the coast, they rounded a point where Jacques ordered the men to cut the engine and drop the anchor in the lee of the wind. They were fortunate that the spring winds tended to be from the south; here they would be able to take a short break in safety. All were happy for the break and hungry. Smitty prepared Mr. Jonas's Cargo a wonderful meal that was even more appreciated after their lengthy, cramped wagon ride.

Jonas approached Jacques. "Reverend Bailey has told me of you's wonderful work both here and back in da South."

As they shook hands, Jacques explained, "I guess both of us are Southerners who somehow got stuck up here in this cold winter." They smiled at their shared plight.

Jonas explained his connection to the BFG letters Jacques had noticed on the cartons. "Benning Freight Goods is da company my boss uses ta cover movin' my peoples to Canada. I's met Colonel Benning in a terrible battle in Virgini' several years back. I rescued him and now he helps me rescue others. Mr. Jacques, does youse know why dis ship be named *Glory*?"

"No, I've not been told that story."

Jonas smiled. "They's another meanin' to BFG, youse know? They's a song we's all sing called 'Bound for Glory' to help us a keepin' on in our quest to Freedom. When we's see da BFG letters, we know Benning Freight Goods is carryin' Cargo dat's 'Bound for Glory.' They's another song too, called, 'Follow the Drinkin' Gourd'."

Jacques eyes lit up. "I know that one. It's about following the North Star. You see, I've been guided by that same North Star all my life; I inherited knowledge of it from my father. You may be interested to know how I became captain of *Glory*. This past winter I was kidnapped by some bounty hunters. I was rescued by my first mate here, Arch. We thought it was over, but then they blew-up and burned my ship while it was in dry-dock for repairs. It was named *L' Étoile Polaire*. In French, that means *The North Star*.

Now Jonas's eyes got real big; he took Jacques' hand with both of his. "That was a tragic way for us'ens ta meet. But I sees God's hand in all of this, and I knows yose'all be rightly blessed."

Just then Darlene approached with plates of food for them. "Come you big talkers, now it's your turn to eat. If this food doesn't all disappear, Smitty will be up here to find out why not!"

Both men smiled, and Jonas tipped his hat to Darlene.

"This," Jacques said with his arm around Darlene's waist, "This is the best of my many blessings!"

Darlene, too, smiled, reached up, and planted a kiss on Jacques' blushing cheek.

26

GLORY PULLED INTO the dock at Northport. The crew scurried about obtaining new provisions. They would not be staying here long. Jonas was busy with his Cargo. Some were hidden in the BFG crates; some were in the bulkhead's hidden spaces. New boxes were loaded from the dock. All were carefully packed and secured in the small hold. Jacques pulled Jonas aside.

"How many persons are we carrying? These are also BFG boxes? More Cargo?"

Jonas assured Jacques these were part of the diversion, for Colonel Benning transported other supplies to the scattered communities and logging camps around Northern Michigan. Their main destination was Clam River. There, three small narrow-gauge railroads met to supply camps that were situated back away from the water.

Jacques laughed. "We used the same idea up and down the Ohio and the Mississippi. I was told by Mr. Coffin, Darlene's father, that the shipping crate method was first used by a lumber man in Pennsylvania when he shipped by rail car. My bosses and others sort of borrowed and adapted it for boat travel. It works especially well out here, where we don't have as many railroads as they do out east."

Everyone ate, stretched their legs, and prepared to leave the following day. Jacques and Arch spent time studying the charts, for the inland chain of lakes waterway they were to use was entirely new to them and it would be dark. Spring had done its job, and after several weeks of warmth, those inland rivers were free of ice. This trip had to be quick in order to avoid the logs that would soon fill these streams.

When all was ready, *Glory* and her crew set out from Northport. They steamed across the La Grande Traversée and went to the settlement of Elk Rapids. The crew stayed on Glory while the Cargo was gently transferred to a smaller boat, *The Mabel*, for travel on the inland lakes. Captain Hawkins welcomed Jacques aboard. Jacques had prepared to pilot the route but was pleased to have the experienced, Captain Hawkins, at the helm.

All went well except for some errant ice that was stuck in the River Torch and had to be cut loose. They arrived as planned after dark at their destination, Anderson's Store, in the area Jonas called Clam River.

The wind was blowing that night, and the waves rocked *The Mabel*. Jacques was relieved to see the two signal lights at the narrow entrance near Anderson's. All hands were watching and steadying the cargo boxes, some of which had to be lashed to the deck because the hold was so small.

Captain Hawkins skillfully pulled *The Mabel* alongside a wharf on the north side of the Clam River. Captain Hawkins' crew helped unload the BFG boxes. With the rocking, one box tipped precariously toward the water. Jacques had an instant flash back of his first encounter with 'Cargo boxes' at the wharf in Chicago. This night the crew was able to right the box and deliver it safely with the others.

Hoping to speed up their dark of night, clandestine delivery, Jonas had unloaded his valuable Cargo from the boxes while in the hold. They emerged and, as the boat bobbed unsteadily, they held on to each other and the railing. Jacques noticed how carefully and gently Jonas helped his people. Earlier, Jonas had confided to Jacques that the folk in this group were members of his wife's family. One of the women, his wife's sister, was carrying an infant. Jonas and the crew assisted each person over the constantly moving rail and onto the dock. Jacques nervously surveyed the area for intruders. The plan was to hide these fugitives in a tunnel that was hidden in one of the houses behind Anderson's store. The first group off the ship had already disappeared into the darkness accompanied by local supporters.

Jonas was helping the last of his in-laws. A large wave unexpectedly rocked the boat. Jonas's sister-in-law was unsteady; she slipped and fell into Jonas' arms. Jacques gasped as he saw her lose hold of her baby. In an instant the infant fell into the water and disappeared between the wharf and the boat. The mother screamed, and Jonas called for help trying to rescue the baby and quiet the hysterical woman. The entire crew searched frantically but could see nothing in the inky darkness. Inevitably, when they finally located the body, the baby had drowned. The woman collapsed in grief on the wharf holding her dead child.

"We must move away quickly. I know it's difficult, but please, be quiet," Jacques heard Jonas cautioning the woman. One of the other women came and took the child as Jonas helped the bereaved mother to her feet. As he did, she screamed ever so loudly. All, especially Jonas, were fearful that the noise would attract unwanted and dangerous attention. Jacques cringed as he saw Jonas slap the woman hard to quiet her. Her limp body collapsed into his arms. He picked her up, pausing only long enough to look up at Jacques standing helplessly near the rail. Then he hurried off and disappeared into the darkness.

Jacques knew their task was over, and *The Mabel* needed to move out quickly before it attracted more attention. He and Captain Hawkins exchanged signals and *The Mabel* moved away from the wharf. They moved on up Torch Lake to continue their delivery to a settlement at the north end of the lake. *More saw mills needing supplies and equipment,* thought Jacques. *That makes for a great ruse to cover the delivery of our Cargo. But, oh, the tragedy.* He thought of how much risk and danger these desperate fugitives faced every mile of their journey from slavery-hell to Freedom. These fugitives were 90% of the way from Virginia to Freedom and then this tragedy struck. Jacques crossed himself and breathed a prayer.

They returned to Elk Rapids and Jacques quietly thanked their new partners from *The Mabel.* Jacques was relieved to reconnect with Darlene who had stayed with the crew to watch over *Glory.* As they rested with a hot cup of tea, he shared the sad story of Jonas's family. "It was an impossible task. It would have been difficult to save the child in broad daylight, but in the dark, impossible," he muttered. He held his head in his hands as Darlene moved closer to comfort him in his grief.

Before Captain Jacques and the *Glory* crew left Elk Rapids, they loaded some materials to be delivered to Chicago via Northport. They secured more provisions and set out back across La Grande Traversée to Northport. The trip progressed normally under gray, threatening clouds. All were pleased that the clouds held back their rain or snow, either of which would be possible during this season. They arrived back in Northport to their friends who had been worried about their trip.

"All went fairly well," Jacques reported as he looked at Darlene with a knowing glance.

Turning to Payson, Jacques inquired, "Where's Arch?"

Payson explained Arch had been called back to Benzonia to help transport the last small group of fugitives from Reverend Bailey. He further explained that the pressure from bounty hunters had increased, and Reverend Bailey was extremely anxious about the safety of their valuable Cargo. Now, with the ice out of the bay south of Northport, the new proposal was to meet Arch and his Cargo in two days. Arch would bring the Cargo overland for a short distance to a river that flows north into the bay. Arch's canoes would then take them the second part of the trip, and they would rendezvous with Jacques at a dockage just west of the Traverse settlement.

Everyone appreciated the day of rest before they were to meet Arch. However, the crew still needed to move the regular cargo from Elk Rapids on its way to Chicago. Fortunately, an early schooner was loading at the same dock and had agreed to take Jacques' cargo to Chicago along with its lumber. Mack had been concerned and needed the day to tear a leaky valve apart and return it to working condition. Jacques had listened intently to Mack's description of the valve problem, but in the end, he just nodded and let Mack work his miracle with the machine.

The next day, with a load of supplies to camouflage the Cargo they would pick up, *Glory* moved from the dock. It was to be a quick trip, just three hours down the bay. Jacques and Darlene enjoyed their time together. It was the first time in a long time they actually could talk. Darlene looked to the right and pointed out the two-flag signal on a short dock that seemed camouflaged along the forested shore. As they slowed, Arch appeared on the dock.

"It's Arch," Darlene said, "and more." With that she left the wheelhouse and flew down the ladder in a hurry. *What got into her?* Jacques wondered, but he became involved navigating the ship in close to the small dock. Arch and his Cargo clambered aboard. The fugitive family of five was hustled into the hold and given food before they were stowed away. Jacques quickly reversed engines, pulled away, and steered *Glory* out into the bay for the trip back north.

Arch and Darlene joined Jacques in the wheelhouse, bringing him up-to-date regarding recent happenings. They explained that Reverend Bailey had heard of Jacques' encounter with the Southern bounty hunters at the Aurl dock. The Reverend was concerned that those men might be the same bounty hunters who had been nosing around his school. Reverend Bailey was sure they were involved in the murder of his friend, Sheriff Marshall, especially since the murder had occurred in Aurl. He was beside himself. Arch eventually was able to reassure him the fugitives would be safe. With the ice out of the bay and out of the Boardman waterway that fed into the bay from the south, Arch was able to travel overland a short trek with the fugitives and then canoe them on up the river. He and the fugitives met *Glory* without incident. Arch was happy to report that everything had gone as planned.

"What do you think had the Reverend so upset?" Darlene inquired.

Arch shook his head, paused, and then spoke. "I think it must have been those same two bounty hunters."

Right then Mack interrupted to report that his engine repair seemed to be working well. He wanted to increase the ship's speed on the return trip in order to make a test run. Jacques agreed.

Arch jumped up. "I need to retrieve my gear. I'll be right back." He ran off down the ladder as Jacques revved up the engine.

Darlene spoke up. "Arch has another passenger, and I know who it is." Confused Jacques just looked at her.

Arch returned shortly to the wheelhouse.

"Where did you go in such a rush?" Jacques asked.

"Oh, I went to retrieve some valuable cargo of my own."

Jacques turned to Arch thinking he meant more fugitives, but stopped when he saw the grin on Arch's face. Arch then walked over to the hatch, swung it open, and said, "Yes, very valuable cargo." In walked Star with an equally big grin, followed by Darlene who had been bursting, wanting to let Jacques in on the secret before Arch could get a chance.

"What a surprise! Actually, I knew something was up when I saw Arch's broad grin." Jacques stepped over and gave Star a big hug.

Darlene was right behind her. "Hey, what about a hug for me?"

The four friends laughed together as *Glory* picked up speed and hurried home to Northport. But where was home for any of them?

Arriving back in Northport, even before they could unload their Cargo, they found the town in a buzz with news. Reverend Smith ran up to the ship holding a newspaper with a headline that shouted: *Lee Surrenders*!

Their happiness was tempered with a pause and a confusing question: *What happens next?*

⎯⎯ᴄ

27

THEIR RETURN TO Northport could almost be called shocking. The war was over! This was the biggest news imaginable. So many lives had been wrapped up in the work of helping fugitives. What would they do now? Reverend Smith would go on ministering with his settlement in Northport. Reverend Bailey would go on to develop his school. What about Jacques? He had never known any other life. Years of dedication and danger could not end so quickly, could they? Jacques' mind was reeling along with those of his partners.

Reverend Smith passed around the Chicago paper that had come to them on another early steamer which had arrived that day. The paper was dated April 10, 1865, nearly a week before. The words were repeated again and again, "The war is over! The war is over! " Reverend Smith raised his hand to get everyone's attention.

"I don't know if you are praying people, but we need to stop for a minute to give thanks. Be thankful this horrible war is finally over." 'Amen' was heard throughout the small crowd.

Then someone spoke the question on each person's mind, "Reverend, what's going to happen? I mean happen here, to us?"

"I'm just like you. I don't know exactly what this means. How it will affect our work will become clearer soon. But right now, this I know: Nothing has changed. That is because we still have fugitives to transport," he motioned to *Glory*, "including the Harrison family below deck right now. There are others still in transit hoping to get to Freedom. They have suffered long and hard. We'll be beside them and help them until there are no more coming our way."

"Here, here," said Jacques. "For now, let's get back to work. Arch, will you take the ladies, find Mary and Payson, and get them settled for the night? We have much to discuss, but that can wait until later. On your way, please tell Mack I need him."

Turning to address Reverend Smith, he said, "Send your people to take our Cargo to safe shelter tonight. Care for them. They must be exhausted from their journey, especially through this horrid winter."

Each dispersed to his task. Jacques and Mack tied and secured *Glory* at the dock. Mack assisted the fugitive Cargo out of the hold and onto the covered wagon carrying them to their shelter. The crew relaxed some. Smitty prepared a special meal to celebrate the war's end and everyone settled together in the cramped quarters. As they ate, Jacques spoke, "Men, I've no idea what the end of the war means to us and our work. We still have fugitives stranded mid-way between their old lives and Freedom. They still need our help. I have no idea how many there are or how few. *Glory* here has been a blessing in place of our beloved friend, *L'Étoile Polaire.*" He paused in an obviously emotional moment. "The work you and I do has been eternally blessed. As it comes to a welcome close with the end of the fighting, you will forever feel in your hearts a warm sense of accomplishment. Yes, we've taken fugitives from Hell, and now they're in sight of Freedom." A cheer went up from the men for their Captain, and for all of those people who'd found Freedom.

After dinner the crew dispersed. Jacques knew they'd be back on Lake Michigan the next day, so he returned to the wheelhouse to review his maps. He was worried about the clouds he'd seen before dark, but he'd deal with them later. He turned off the lamp, took down the lantern, and walked off the dock in search of his friends. Though he was tired, he knew his mind, full of questions, would not let him find the sleep he wished for that night.

The weather blew in rough, so *Glory* stayed in Northport for several days. The season for snow was gone. However, late spring thunder storms often stirred up heavy waves. The layover was helpful, not just for relaxing but for planning. No one knew what was next, but they had always been a team. In the back of their minds were the obvious questions: What is our future? Together? Apart? In the North? Back to the South?

During the weather delay, a packet of letters was received from Darlene's father. In Cincinnati, Mr. Coffin was closer to the situation, so his thoughts and directions were highly appreciated. He had been in communication with Reverend Bailey in Benzonia. The three, including Reverend Smith, had been the leaders of this western movement of fugitive slaves. The men shared their thoughts and plans. The letters exchanged with Reverend Bailey told of his joy at helping Star connect with Arch; he wished them well. His communication also confirmed what Arch and Jacques had feared. His operation in Benzonia had been attacked by the bounty hunters. They had thought they would do great harm by burning the barn. But Arch had removed all the valuable Cargo. So, ironically, when they torched the barn, they actually destroyed any evidence the bounty hunters could use against the Bailey's. Reverend Bailey praised Arch for his help, then added he saw God's hand at work through him.

Regardless of what happened, one task remained. They had the Harrison family of fugitives to get to Freedom. On the fourth day, the weather cleared and preparations were made for them to cross La Grande Traversée again. They set out under bright skies, and the trip moved quickly. Once they were underway, Arch joined Jacques in the wheelhouse. Jacques greeted his friend with a broad smile but continued studying his maps.

After a few minutes, Arch spoke. "This is the part of the country were I began my work some years ago." Moving over to the map, Arch pointed out their destination and went on. "Many of my brothers live in this area here," he said, pointing out Cross Village and L'Arbre Croche. "As I've told you before, our people have always had a close kinship with the Fugitives. We are both fugitive people in this country, I'm afraid." He sighed deeply and continued. "Chief An-ho-ak, a friend of my father, was recruited by Reverend Smith to handle this last part of the journey. Reverend Smith will see the Cargo safely to here," (Pointing it out.) "and my brothers will transport them from that point.

"I was just a young, wild buck with little knowledge. My father was very wise and sent me here to work with our brothers from L'Arbre Croche. That was many years ago." Looking back to the map he went on. "We call this La Petite Traversée, or 'short trip,' because the bay is narrow, but there is more to the phrase than that. We Native people have done most of our travel by canoe, which is dangerous on any of the big lakes. We preferred not to go to Michilimackinac from the west because that area contains some of the most dangerous sailing waters in Lake Michigan. We know of an inland water route that takes us very near Michilimackinac, but from the east side. You see it is just a small walk, thus, La Petite Traversée…"

Arch paused and Jacques noticed a smile and a twinkle in his friend's eye. "…A short trip of only a few miles, and we hook up with Crooked Lake in this Chain of Lakes." (Pointing out again on the map) "See here, take the Crooked River to the Burt Lake and through a connecting stream called the Indian River. Then on into Indian Lake which is emptied by the Che-boy-na-gan River which empties into Lake Huron. Look how close it is to Michilimackinac. It is only six miles up the coast to our destination, the village of Freedom."

Arch stepped back to see if Jacques had absorbed all this information. Jacques' fingers traced along the map over the route Arch had described.

Arch pointed to a spot along Lake Huron and explained, "Freedom is a community established by freed blacks and fugitive slaves that has been a main station for moving people from Michigan over to Canada. There are over a hundred permanent residents who live there, and they are very dedicated to their work. It has been a real honor for me to work with them."

Jacques shook his head in disbelief. "I remember you explained that to me before we arrived in Chicago. I'd thought then that the phrase 'going on to Freedom' meant going from slavery to freedom in Canada. But you told me it is also a destination. Now we are very close. I look forward to seeing the real place."

Arch smiled. "Does it remind you of anywhere else? Think way back years ago when we worked together on the Ohio River."

Jacques looked up with a surprised smile. "The town of New Liberty, Indiana. Well, I'll be. We've come full circle, my friend."

Glory arrived safely near the end of the bay. There Arch pointed to a several obscure warehouses and they slowed near one; Jacques smiled at the one labeled 'Northern Freight.' *Just like before*, he thought to himself. They were pleased to see two flags signaling safety. They didn't tie up, but carefully delivered the Harrison family to Arch's friends.

Arch exchanged some quick words with them in Ojibway, waved, and jumped back on the ship. The crew pushed away with the pike poles they'd used to hold the ship during the transfer. Steaming away, Arch directed *Glory* across the bay to another dock where it tied up. Arch went inside and returned with another man as Jacques approached the ship's rail.

"This is our new Captain. Mr. Henderson, meet Jacques Bateau. Jacques, Mr. Henderson was a mentor of mine years ago, often keeping me in line. "

"Captain Bateau, a Frenchman," and he smiled. "Nice to meet you. Good to see you, too, Arch. You give me far too much credit. Anyway, you've been gone too long." He patted Arch on the back and continued, "Let's get you unloaded quickly so we can sit over coffee and catch up." They smiled and walked off.

Though it was well past midday, they didn't get their regular cargo off-loaded until dark. Jacques decided to wait until morning to return to Northport. He and Arch ate, enjoyed some 'old times' reminiscing with Mr. Henderson, and turned in after midnight for an easy voyage back.

Their arrival in Northport was wonderful because both Jacques and Arch were greeted by their favorite ladies.

"Welcome home," was mixed with hugs, smiles and kisses. "We'll tell you more over dinner," Darlene added, "for we've received additional correspondence from Reverend Bailey and my father."

Arch and Jacques secured the ship, and the four friends reunited at Reverend Smith's quarters.

28

I N NORTHPORT, THERE was more news about the end of the war. People
everywhere were excited and looking forward to loved ones' return.
That night was spent discussing the future. Reverend Bailey's letter told
of further communication with Mr. Coffin. Both sent their warm greet-
ings and love to the North Country. Jacques could tell Darlene missed
her family by the way she looked when the letter mentioned her father.
Jacques pondered what he, or rather 'they,' would do when their work
was over. He had little time to sit and think. They still had several
trips ahead and Cargo to transport. *Glory* was also busy with a growing business moving regular cargo. As the war veterans returned, the
government was encouraging development of wilderness areas with gifts
of land. Settlers would be given one hundred acres if they would stay on
the land and farm it. Many took advantage of the offer, and small communities were developing and growing. Each of them needed supplies
to prosper and *Glory* was establishing a regular supply route both north
and south of Northport.

Jacques and the crew talked about staying to take advantage of this
growing opportunity. Jonathan and Peter shivered at the thought and
voiced their plans to return to the warmer South. Jacques was especially
curious about Arch's plans. Arch and Star were, as usual, very quiet
and didn't share much. Jacques sought out Mack, for he'd become very

popular with the crew and had expressed some interest in getting his Captain's license. Everyone knew one thing for sure. Change was coming quickly. There was a sense of anticipation in the air. But what was it mixed with? Sadness? Or melancholy? Or hope? Or excitement? The answer varied from person to person.

"It's hard to imagine our work ending," Jacques told Darlene one evening. "This is the only job I've ever known."

"Yes, I know," she replied reflectively. "At least you are a Captain and could continue running *Glory* if you chose to. But I don't know what to do. My father has been involved in helping fugitives from my earliest memory. At first, he kept his work secret from me and the family. One thing he insisted on was that I get my schooling. But after studying, I would sneak downstairs to listen to him and his friends make plans.

"One night I hid away on a wagon that was going out to pick up some fugitives. We bumped along through the woods somewhere near the river. Finally, the wagon stopped and all was silent. I got scared. Then I heard the sound of an owl. I heard my father, who was driving the wagon, answer with his own owl call. I thought his imitation was terrible and almost giggled out loud. Then I heard the sound of people moving through the leaves and bushes. Someone grabbed the tarp I was under and threw it back. I saw my father's face in the dim lantern light. He was furious! He wanted to scold me, but he had to keep quiet and whisper. All I remember him saying was, 'Wait 'til we get home, young lady.'

"Soon the wagon was loaded with many people crowded into the small space. A lady pushed next to me in the dark, and I could tell she was holding a restless, crying baby. When I reached over to soothe the child, it settled immediately. Then I realized the woman had another child as well. So I reached up, took the child that was next to me, and rocked it. We could barely see each other, and we certainly didn't know each other. I don't know what possessed me to take charge of her baby.

"We rode on for some time and stopped finally. I had no idea where we were. My father pulled back the canvas and saw me and this woman nestled together with two sleeping babies. He told me later that seeing us there really melted his heart. I think he knew right away, I would be working with him from then on. But now what? You and I have had this life and only this life for years. Now what am I to do?"

Deep in thought, they sat in silence watching the fading light of the fire.

An urgent sound on the cabin door roused them from their daydreams. Jacques quickly jumped up. He pulled the door open to find a young man leaning heavily on the door jamb with a limp woman in his arms. Jacques could see they were both badly injured, and the man was bleeding under his right eye.

"Can you...?" The man stammered as he slumped against the door. Darlene was immediately at Jacques' side. She and Jacques gathered the couple and brought them into the room. Darlene lay the young girl on the bed, as Jacques helped the man to a chair.

"Here, sip this warm tea," Jacques offered the man, along with a towel to stop the bleeding.

Darlene whispered in his ear, "I'll get Arch," and hurried out the door.

The young lady was unconscious. Jacques didn't know if she was wounded, or sick, or maybe even dead. The young man stammered, "We...are...Quakers."

"Take it slow, sir," Jacques re-assured him.

"We were beaten." He stopped and sipped some tea. He seemed to be gathering some strength. "We were beaten by some men. They must have tracked us. They beat our companions worse, and..." He dropped his head on his arm atop the table.

"Easy now," Jacques spoke, patting the man's shoulder. "Don't try to talk yet."

"But, you must.... You must go. Some may be...dead." With that he again collapsed on his arm and sobbed.

Just then, Darlene returned with Arch and Star.

"You go with Arch," she said to Jacques. "There's trouble. Star and I will care for this couple."

Jacques grabbed his coat and followed Arch. They hurried down the lane toward Reverend Smith's house. As they turned the corner, they saw fire. Fortunately, the men of Northport had the fire fairly under control by the time the two got there.

Jacques pulled at Arch's shoulder. "What's going on?"

Arch pulled Jacques over to the closest porch where two men and a woman huddled. Payson and Mary were tending to them. The men had bandages on their heads and one man's arm was in a sling.

"Where is...?" Arch asked, and Payson pointed inside. He and Jacques entered the small store and saw Reverend Smith with several others gathered around a wood stove.

"We've got to leave now to be safe," one man said.

"No bunch of hot heads is goin' to push me out," said another as he lifted his rifle in the air.

"Now, now, please calm down," Reverend Smith implored. "Here are our friends, the Captain and Mate of *Glory*. Make room for them."

The group opened to let Jacques and Arch into the circle. Jacques surveyed the group who were raging with anger. Arch's sage words to him from when the L'Étoile Polaire burned suddenly came back to him. *Rage is an angry wind...*

Someone in the circle spoke up. "Reverend, no offense, but those ruffians know of your secret work helping the fugitives. I'm a 'feared they'll burn us all!"

"Yup, I'm packin' up my wife and kids! We're heading to the Traverse Settlement tonight. We'll be safer there." He spit a wad into the spittoon and started to walk out.

"Gentlemen, Gentlemen. Let's review what we know. That will help Captain Jacques and Arch here decide what to do." The Reverend explained, "A settler from out on Kirby Hill rode into town about two hours ago screaming. Before I could get any information, two other men rode in, obviously chasing him. They pulled up and yelled, 'You nigger lovers are goin' a burn!' They then lit a torch and threw it into the Hall's cabin. You saw it burning over yonder. The family all got out, but..." He dropped his head, "there were two of our special Cargo hidden in the basement." He took another deep breath and added, "I'm afraid both of those men perished."

"Ya, and they'll do the same to all of us, 'cause of this illegal work y'all's been doin'!" someone yelled. He was restrained by two others as the Reverend continued.

"We have good word that the men fled south. But we fear they may have harmed some folks out at Hawking's Corner."

"Were they a young Quaker couple?" Jacques interjected.

"Yes," The Reverend turned his attention to Jacques. Jacques proceeded to tell of the injured couple who had stumbled into his cabin.

"Darlene and Star are tending to them now. Were there more at Hawking's Corner?"

The Reverend's hand went to his mouth and his eyes widened.

"Say no more," Jacques said. "Get horses," he said to Arch who left on the run.

"And you men, hush that panic talk! You organize a guard and watch detail. At daylight you'll check all the settlements and families. We are in this together and together we stay secure." He looked around and stood eye to eye with each man there. Jacques was a tall, strong, imposing man. The other men felt his strength and agreed.

"Yes," Reverend Smith said. "Come now. You, Harold, make a list of the men in the settlement, and we'll organize a schedule right now."

"Good thinking," Jacques said and ran out the door. He met Arch coming up the street pulling two horses. They mounted and headed out of town to the south. Arch knew the area and led the way. It was not far to the farm, and there they saw the remains of trouble. A dead cow lay in the driveway with a helpless calf trying to muzzle its cold, lifeless mother. The drive led up to a dark house on the right. They dismounted and approached the farm house warily. Everything seemed quiet. The door to the small frame house was open, but no one stirred inside. Jacques grabbed a lantern from a hook by the door and lit it. The light shown on chaos. Someone had purposely thrown the contents of every cupboard on the floor.

He and Arch returned to the yard and found another dead animal near the barn. They walked toward it and stopped abruptly. They listened; they heard something. They approached the small barn door, pushed it in, and heard the squeak of a rusty hinge. Their light shown on a grizzly scene. Arch hurried to two Negro men tied to the center post. Jacques quickly climbed to the loft and cut the rope releasing the limp body of a young man into the arms of the others. The two men huddled on the ground holding the body. One of the men sobbed as he brushed the dirt from the dead child's hair.

"He's ma only, my's flesh and blood. I's promised his mama we'd be free together. She died and we buried her back on the trail near a week ago. My boy...," he sobbed. Jacques felt anguish for these men. He knew what they had suffered to get this far.

Suddenly, they heard the sound of horses from the road. Everyone froze in panic. Jacques doused the lantern. He and Arch unholstered their pistols and stood ready at the door.

"Hello there. Anyone here? Jacques or Arch, are you here?" They heard a friendly voice from outside.

Relieved, they welcomed two townsfolk. They helped Jacques and Arch take the two Negro men and the body to Northport. There the men were sheltered and their wounds were tended. The young boy's body was prepared for burial by Mary and her mother, Reverend Smith's wife.

Jacques felt great remorse. He had been fortunate over the many years of his work not to experience many tragedies such as this. The death of his father lingered sadly in his mind. He wondered. *Why at this time when the war is finally over? All the slaves are freed. Yet, still the anger persists. For how long? And how many more children will we have to bury?* He hung his head in sadness.

29

OVER THE NEXT few days, there was much hustle and bustle. It was imperative the Cargo be moved from Northport immediately. Messages were received from Reverend Bailey informing Jacques of another family of five arriving soon. All the fugitives were gathered into safe quarters. The young Quaker couple gradually improved, and, with the help of some sympathetic friends, resumed work at their farm. However, they did return to the settlement each night for safety. Eventually, they would recover, but it would take time.

The crew hurried to get *Glory* ready. There was a deep sadness in the community as they steamed out the next day. They departed before the hurried funeral of the young boy and the two men who died in the fire at the Hall's cabin. Jacques and *Glory* headed toward Reverend Bailey's area near Frankfort. Arriving at night at the Aurl dock, they were relieved to see the two-lantern safe signal. They loaded the last of the human Cargo and stowed them below. They steamed on the short distance to Frankfort and delivered a load of goods so no one would be the wiser about the real reason for their visit.

By the time they returned to Northport, all was rather calm. The local people had decided not to report the marauding murderers for fear of exposing their transport business. Instead, they informed a deputy friend who lived in the Leland fishing area. They asked him to quietly do whatever he could. He informed them later that a group of four men had gotten into a fight in a local bar which ended badly for them. The Native fishermen did not appreciate their prejudiced attitudes and their talk of 'dumb injuns.' The four were last seen naked, staked, and tied to trees along the shore. It had been a fitting ending; they would receive little sympathy from the Northport community.

With new provisions secured, *Glory* prepared to leave for La Petite Traversée. The Cargo, now numbering only seven, were loaded into hidden compartments. Cartons of supplies to be delivered to the lumber camp supply depot had also been loaded. Darlene and Star informed the men that they were coming along and prepared makeshift quarters for themselves in the rear hold area. The men were astonished and protested half-heartedly, but were secretly pleased with the new arrangements.

Jacque thought to himself, *Is this the last journey? Are these the last fugitives? The war is over and so is the Underground Railroad. We still work to do and no time to worry about what comes next.* Jacques and his crew launched *Glory* and steamed out on what Jacques thought might to be their last journey across the La Grande Traversée. Since the recent attack in Northport, there was tension, yet hope, mixed with the unknown. Everyone dealt with this final chapter in his or her own way. Their mission was not yet complete, and the danger of the trip kept everyone's senses keen and focused. All were relieved when the trip proceeded on schedule.

As they neared the Crooked River Traverse, another ship sat at the dockage. The two-flag signal flew openly and *Glory* pulled in alongside the other ship. They were greeted and ushered into the building where several men had gathered. Jacques and Arch looked about in wonder. A man they had met on previous visits stepped forward, greeted them, and introduced the other men present.

"Here is our problem, gentlemen. As our job comes to an end, there is a rush to finish transporting fugitives. We don't want to leave anyone stranded. Captain Jacques here has a group of seven persons to move on to Freedom. This is Captain Ecorse." At the introduction, a stocky, bearded, weathered man stepped forward and shook hands with Jacques. "Captain Ecorse just arrived this morning with the last overland group of five who came up the Boardman waterway. At dawn, they were sent on their way to Freedom. Our dilemma is simple; we have Cargo, but we have no Native crew to transport them."

Jacques looked at Arch and the two exchanged a knowing glance. "Excuse me, Sir," Jacques interrupted. "I think we can solve your dilemma. My first mate here, Arch, is a cousin of a member of your transport crew now on the Crooked River Traverse. We have at least three experienced canoeists and enough crew to keep *Glory* safe while they're gone. I think the urgency is upon us." With that, he briefly explained the recent tragedy at Northport. "So you see why we need to get underway immediately." All agreed, and Jacques and Arch left to prepare.

Arch took care of the equipment and arranged for the transportation. Jacques went back aboard *Glory* and explained the new plans to Darlene and Star.

"What?" Darlene exclaimed. "I've never even been in a canoe!"

Smiling, Star stepped forward and said, "Darlene, it's easy. I'll teach you. It will be a new adventure for us to share." Darlene gradually calmed down.

Jacques was pleased to see how the girls' friendship had grown. He likened them to himself and Arch. He smiled; it was warm feeling.

"We'll pack quickly," Star said and pulled Darlene with her to keep her busy so she wouldn't worry.

In this area so far to the north, development had been very sparse. This portion of the route had seen minimal trouble over the years. The group could move about easily with less need for secrecy. With Arch's keen knowledge of the area, they covered the short portage over to the Crooked River rendezvous site. There they were met by two of Arch's Native brothers. It had been a long time, so they were glad to see him again. Introductions were made and several canoes were removed from storage.

Arch explained his brothers were surprised to see another group of fugitives. They had just sent out the previous group of five two days earlier. Arch and Jacques were relieved to see they were using a Voyager canoe which was larger, and, though harder to paddle, allowed more room for hauling. The fugitives they were transporting were very nervous about the canoes, but Arch and Jacques eventually calmed them. Darlene, too, needed much encouragement from both Jacques and Star before she boarded.

They got under way and made it to their camp near the Indian River for the first night. All welcomed food and rest. Many shoulders ached, sore from the long day's paddling. Although they anticipated no problems on this route, Jacques and Arch were vigilant and set up a rotating guard schedule.

The next days were cool and cloudy. Sore shoulders continued to bother them, so Jacques and Arch welcomed paddling help from two of the older Negro men. They were able to set up a rotation of paddlers and, with time, their aching shoulders felt better. Rain interrupted day three, but it was a warm spring rain and no one was bothered. Passengers and gear were kept secure and dry under tarps, but still progress was slowed. Yet it did not dampen their spirits. Several men sang the old trail songs, celebrating because they were finally 'in sight of Freedom.'

That evening the rain stopped and the fire blazed, drying out damp clothes. It was very tiring work and most of the group had gone to sleep. Darlene sat with Jacques discussing the trip. Jacques began, "I've been thinking."

"I'm relieved to know my Captain and leader thinks," Darlene laughed, flashing her sly smile at Jacques.

"I'm glad you are relieved," he shot back, enjoying the ease of their conversation. As they approached the end of not only this journey, but their years of work assisting in the transport of fugitives, they hoped their years of tension and stress were now behind them.

"Seriously now, what comes next? Do you want to return to your family in Cincinnati?" Jacques asked.

There was no quick sarcasm this time. Darlene turned the question back on him. "Do you want to return to New Orleans and work with your mother and Burt?"

No answers came quickly for either of them, as they thoughtfully gazed into the fire.

"Look up there," Jacques pointed. "We've always followed the North Star. *N'oublie pas L'Étoile Polaire*, my father would say. I am comfortable to let that same wisdom guide us to our next decision."

"I can agree with that," Darlene said and reached for Jacques hand. "Whatever we decide, I'd like to do it together."

Jacques smiled feeling secure that *L'Étoile Polaire* would indeed guide them throughout their lives.

The trip on up the interconnected lakes progressed well, and they were met by a greeting party as soon as they got to Lake Huron. The greeters, a group of Negro men who were dressed more like Natives and paddling canoes, had obviously adapted to the ways of the North. They paid special attention to the new arrivals, putting all fears and anxiety to rest. All moved together the short distance up the shore to Freedom. The weather was good and they arrived to a joyous welcome.

Another of Arch's friends greeted him for a grand reunion. Hugs, back slapping, and storytelling continued, all in Ojibway, of course. The highlight was when Arch called the shy Star to him and introduced her to his friends. As they were teased, Arch and Star both blushed. The warm feeling of family filled the air.

Jacques and Darlene busied themselves with the gear and other's personal belongings.

"Why don't the fugitives just stay here in Freedom now that the war is over and they have been freed?" Darlene asked Jacques.

"I think that's complicated." Jacques paused in his work to consider her question. "Some are to join family in Ontario and must go there. Most, however, simply do not believe the news of their freedom and are fearful they will still be chased by bounty hunters. I expect it will take some time before that good news sinks in. As we have seen, it's unbelievable to many that they made it here to Freedom. To them, it's inconceivable that they are free to go anywhere."

"I see what you mean," Darlene said thoughtfully.

Some of the new people found family members already in Freedom, and they went off together. The leaders in Freedom had developed a wonderfully detailed, complex system, so soon all were somehow connected and moved on to shelter. They were in Freedom, but for some, one more journey lay ahead, the one to Canada.

As Jacques was retrieving the last of the gear from their recent trip, he heard a deep voice behind him.

"Captain Jacques, 'tis good to see y'all again."

Jacques jumped up in surprise. "Jonas, what...? Darlene! It's Jonas. Why are you here?" The three shook hands and delighted in a wonderful reunion.

Jonas shared his story. "I was da leader of dat group that come just before y'all. This is da last o' ma kin done come to Freedom!"

Jacques was amazed and said, "Jonas, do you remember what you told me when we last parted?"

Jonas shrugged his shoulders and shook his head no.

"You said you knew God was in this plan. I believe your God has brought us together again."

All nodded in agreement and walked off to join the others in celebration.

⎯ϛ

30

THERE WAS A mixture of excitement, fear, doubt, and hope among the people in Freedom. The war was over! The Emancipation Proclamation had been issued! All that was wonderful, but still the question remained: *What now?* Many of the fugitives did not trust the news. They still feared their bondage in the South and were on their way to Canada where they felt they would be safe. They were anxious to move on. The good people of Freedom made all the arrangements and former slaves left for Canada every day.

Jacques and Darlene were also excited by the joyous goal of Freedom. Arriving at Freedom symbolized their whole life's journey. They had been a small part of many people's journey to Freedom. What did it mean now? They hadn't thought much of the future, but had simply continued the work they felt was so deeply important. Arriving in this place was for them a kind of freedom, a time to make decisions about the rest of their lives.

Jacques, Darlene, Arch, and Star helped around the Freedom camp wherever they could. They gathered the canoes and gear and helped Arch's relatives move them back toward home. Mostly, the four moved around in a state of confusion. They were looking at an uncertain future. They were feeling unsettled and nervous.

One night as they sat around a fire in the lodge where they stayed, Jonas walked in. "Mind if'n I's join y'all?"

"Of course not," Jacques replied quickly and pulled up a chair for their friend.

"I be wantin' to stop on by fo I be leavin' tomorrow." Smiling, Jonas looked around at his new friends. He admired them for their selfless work on behalf of his people.

Jacques spoke up. "We were discussing some ideas of what we might do next just as you came in."

"Where will you go, Jonas?" Darlene asked. "You said you had transported all your family out of the South?"

Jonas nodded in agreement and took a deep breath. "Well, I be going back to Antrim County."

"Antrim? Where we left you on that dock near Torch Lake?" Jacques asked.

"But why there?" Darlene said.

"Y'all remember that awful night? Jacques and Arch were there, but y'all left in a hurry. Remember da baby falling in da water?" Jonas paused.

"It all happened so fast, and the boat needed to move away quickly. I think Arch, you might have been below securing other cargo." Jacques was thoughtful, trying to recall. "What happened after we left?"

"Well, da baby done died and we's hurried to bury da chile in that there tunnel we was hidin' in. The chile's mother was my wife's sister, and day both be cryin' and cryin'. But da next night we be ready to move on by wagon. All was quiet and we be only gone a short way when da lady be jumpin' up hittin' and a screamin'. She be yellin' about never leavin' her baby. I be tryin' to get 'holt o' her, so's I could get her quiet."

"Yes," Jacques remembered. "That was the last thing I saw you do. Then you picked her up and disappeared into the darkness."

Jonas shook his head in disbelief. "It was mighty bad. Me's to hit a woman like that. Awful. But we be needin' ta be quiet."

"You only did what you had to do," Jacques said, trying to comfort his friend.

Jonas looked up and replied, "Thank you fo' y'alls understandin' but I was near to do it again when she hits me wife real hard. I'd be concerned mo 'bout my wife and went to help her, when, sho' 'nuff, her sister be jumpin' from da wagon and run off screamin', 'I'll never leave ma baby!'

"My wife be scramblin' out and be tryin' to follow, but it be dark. It was 'portent to be quiet so's we couldn't be hollerin'. Besides, I be responsible and needin' to move on wit' da others. We gots in da wagon and moved on to da next shelter, arrivein' just at dawn. Da good family hid us in a barn and brung us some food. My wife be very sad. She be cryin' and cryin'. Finally, she tolt me she would not leave her kin, no how. She was fixin' to stay. I be beggin' wit her, but it be no help. The good folk at da station say she be okay to stay with dem. They knew there be a lumber camp needin' a cook. She be safe there 'til I be gittin' back.

"I come on with the folk, and I've made two more trips since then. I be stopin' by and see her when I kin. She be doin' fine but still be cryin' 'bout her sister. So, I gots ta go back to Antrim. We be goin' ta have us a family there some day, some way. I's just want to thank y'all fo' yo work. God love ya, I know. I's be prayin' a blessin' on y'all ev'ry day. By the way, what's you'alls plans?" Jonas asked looking around at his friends.

Each one of them looked at the others. Oddly, Arch was the first to speak. "Star and I are going to return to our families on the reservation. My father is getting older, and he wants my help with the leadership. And…" He paused, smiled, and reached for Star's hand, "And Star has agreed to be my bride. We intend to start a family together."

Smiles and cheers passed among the comrades.

Jacques spoke up. "This must be a theme for all of us. We're moving on, just like the many fugitives we've helped over the years. They were helped on to Freedom and a new beginning. I think that's what we're all seeking. Jonas here is going to stop traipsing back and forth from Virginia in the dark of night. He's going to settle down. That's his new beginning! Arch, you know how close we've been through these years. Now it's time for a change. Maybe you'll become your tribe's next new chief, yes, Chief To-ma-ho. That has a nice ring to it."

Jacques stopped and looked at Darlene. Then she spoke up.

"Today Jacques and I received a letter from my father in Cincinnati. He's informed us of his challenge. He says there's a big need to help the thousands of fugitives now in Canada to resettle. Now that the war is over, some want to come back home to the South. Others have no home to return to but want to return to live in the States. My father and others from the old Underground Railroad are rallying to help in that resettlement. Jacques and I are going to Ontario as soon as we can arrange passage. That's our new beginning!"

"Oh, yes," Jacques interrupted blushing, "this dear woman has agreed to become Mrs. Bateau, so we can work together on our new mission."

Darlene was not to be out done, "And to add to the meaning, we are going to a settlement in Ontario called Dawn. It will be a new day!"

The group was joyful though somewhat sad as they discussed their future plans. No one knew if their paths would cross again, but with the blessing of Jonas' God and with their hope for the future, they celebrated their new directions. Jacques reminded them, "N'oublie pas, L'Étoile Polaire" (Don't forget the North Star). The North Star would continue to guide them all, wherever they might be.

EPILOGUE NOTES FROM THE AUTHOR:

WHILE GOING OVER Jacques' diaries and information he recorded later in his life, this author came across some Indian lore Jacques had included. Arch had recommended that while they wintered on the reservation, Jacques should spend some time listening to the stories of the elders. One particular topic had to do with the area around Arcadia, where they had stopped briefly on their way to Frankfort. Arch had remarked about the crows they saw there.

From what he wrote, Jacques obviously sat at the feet of the elders on several occasions. As would be the custom, these were not question and answer sessions, but times for listening. Possibly his first-mate, Arch, a member of the tribe, may have asked a question. Possibly one elder or a small group of elders were simply sitting around telling stories. We don't know. All we have are some sketches and notes left in Jacques' journals from that winter.

The first recorded notes seem to have come from a question such as: 'Tell us what is so special about the Arcadia area?' This is Jacques' record of the elder's response.

"The area that you speak of is an area of very strong energy and power. Some say 'it has powerful medicine.' I know it is so because I have entered that area on spiritual quests many times, as have my brothers. I, personally, went there to fast and seek my direction as a young leader of this tribe. It was there I was shown my role, not as a Chief but as an interpreter of signs. This area near Arcadia has always been a sacred place for the Indian and an eerie place for our white brothers. They seem not to see the power of those hills. They only focus on what they call 'strange happenings.' We Indians know the area to have spiritual power. When a brother dies, his spirit may linger before it is transported to the other world. A force brings those waiting spirits to the Arcadian hills. I have sat during my many nights of fasting and prayer and watched large spinning clouds of spirits blow through the area and sometimes alight on the ground.

"The presence of such spiritual energy bother's some. Maybe it would bother you? If you get a chance to go there on a spiritual quest, you will see of what I speak. Several of my brothers have dug cave-like shelters on the sand of near-by bald-top hills. Those high, clear areas around Acadia seem to attract much spiritual energy. Maybe there is a force that pulls and holds the spirits there. I do not know, but I do not think so. I believe Arcadia is a special, powerful place that gathers the spirits of those who have died, but it is only a temporary dwelling place. One time I go and see many swirling spirits, but other times only a small number. I believe Arcadia is a scared place where the spirits collect together before they make their great Journey to the great beyond, to the land of *Gitchi Manitou*.

"You asked about the crows. As you spend more time with our people, you will notice how important many large birds are to us. We feel that the large birds come from the highest spirit, which we call

Gitchi Manitou. White man's worship houses use the name *God.* We are thinking alike when we pray to those who possess these names.

"Regarding the crows, they are a majestic animal but not regarded as highly as the eagle. Watch them walk with elegance; their shiny black feathers reveal their regal heritage. The crows of Arcadia are gatherers of lost spirits. Crows group together and bring together the lost spirits they carry to prepare them for their assent. However, the blackness terrifies those who fear the darkness. It may be similar to the fear the white man has for any persons of a different color like your fugitive passengers or us, the Native Indians.

"Some tribes cherish the owl or the hawk. Each of the powerful birds are honored because we believe their strength lets them fly the highest and get the closest to our spiritual leader, *Gitchi Manitou.* Strength, power, beauty, and stamina are all characteristics of the mighty birds that we worship.

"Our cherished bird is the eagle. One of the Ojibway's most holy possessions is an eagle's feather. You may not see many during your stay with us, for we save these cherished feathers to use when we dress for our highest spiritual celebrations and dances. Most of our festivals are in the summer, so you will have to return then, and I will show you of what I speak."

Jacques seems to have been deeply impressed by the spiritualism demonstrated by the Native elders. Upon seeing an eagle in flight, perhaps he was reminded of the paintings on the paddle he had in his youth which included bird images. He must have been influenced enough by those events to write a poem. There was only one other time, when he first left his mother at Isle Polaire, that he wrote poetry. I include his poem here for you to appreciate a more spiritual side of Jacques personality.

WHEN THE EAGLE FLIES

When eyes again look up
Having long been beaten down,
That's when the eagle flies.

When the body moves from under the lash,
With strength hidden as in a stash,
That's when the eagle flies.

Souls cannot long be held down,
Beaten as they've been down to the ground,
That's when the eagle flies.

When worn spirits again have soared,
Lifted to new heights adored,
That's when the eagle flies.

When hope sees light up ahead,
When all seems only dark and dead,
That's when the eagle flies.

The eagle flies and lifts on high
The greatest gift of freedom.
The eagle flies and carries souls
To the greatest gift of freedom.
The eagle flies and the struggling share
The greatest gift of freedom.

Fly. Eagle, Fly!
Yes, Fly, Eagle, Fly!

INFORMATIONAL BIBLIOGRAPHY

<u>Author's Note:</u> This is not meant to be even close to a complete list of re-sources. All I am sharing here are some of the most informational books and web-sites I found helpful. One thing I found exciting was that there are new books being published, new research being done, and renewed inter-est in the Underground Railroad. One troubling thing I sensed was that most of the literature out there is in the children's or young teen areas of the library. This is too exciting a topic to believe it is only children's literature. I encourage you to grow in knowledge of this topic. I have found a great reward in my research of this topic.

Topic One: The Underground Railroad General

Bordewich, Fergus M., <u>Bound for Canaan: The Underground Railroad and the war for the soul of America</u>, Harper-Collins Publishing Co. 2005

Siebat, Rev. William H., <u>The Underground Railroad from Slavery to Freedom </u>(Originally published in 1898), Republished in by Dover Publishing, 2006

Simon, Barbara Brooks, <u>Escape to Freedom</u> National Geographic, Publisher 2004

Swain, Gwenyth, <u>President of the Underground Railroad: The Story of Levi Coffin,</u> Carolrhoda Books of Minneapolis 2001

Tobin, Jacqueline L., <u>From Midnight to Dawn: The Last Tracks of the Underground Railroad</u> New York Doubleday Publishing 2007

Topic Two: Michigan Resources

Ewing, Wallace K., <u>Slaves Soldiers Citizens: African Americans in Northwest Ottawa County</u>, Great Lakes Printing Solutions, Muskegon, Michigan 2011

Mitchell, John C., <u>Grand Traverse in the Civil War Era,</u> Suttons Bay Publications, Suttons Bay, Michigan 2011

Oickle, Alvin F., <u>Jonathan Walker: The Man with the Branded Hand</u> Lorelli Slater Publishing, Everett, MA 1998

**Note: Most books have extensive additional bibliographies and references.

Website Topics – a partial list

Websites abound! The Internet has put so much information at our fingertips, it is impossible to find but a small portion. I will list a few topics that I used in my research. Do a 'search' on any of these and you will find a trove of good information.

Follow the Drinking Gourd

UGRR Illinois – many maps

UGRR Indiana – many maps

UGRR Ohio – especially, Levi Coffin, the Father of the UGRR

Harriet Tubman –

Josiah Henson – especially about Canada Settlements

Other Negro Settlements and Communities in Canada – such as Dawn, or St. Catherine and others

Made in the USA
Middletown, DE
26 February 2023

25671356R00136